"This is bigger than the Breaks. History is *shattered*. And this time, it's all our fault."

Eternity

Matt de la Peña

SCHOLASTIC INC.

For Ryan Byrne, warrior and reader.
— M.d.l.P.

Library of Congress Control Number: Available

ISBN 978-0-545-66770-8
10 9 8 7 6 5 4 3 2 1   14 15 16 17 18

Cover illustration by Michael Heath
Book design by Keirsten Geise
Back cover photography of characters by Michael Frost © Scholastic Inc.

Library edition, September 2014
Printed in China   62

Scholastic US: 557 Broadway · New York, NY 10012
Scholastic Canada: 604 King Street West · Toronto, ON M5V 1E1
Scholastic New Zealand Limited: Private Bag 94407 · Greenmount, Manukau 2141
Scholastic UK Ltd.: Euston House · 24 Eversholt Street · London NW1 1DB

PROLOGUE

THE HEAT from the fire was unbearable as Dak Smyth tried to claw his way out of the elaborate seat belt. Sweat streamed down his face. It soaked his shirt and pants underneath his bulky suit. It even soaked the protective diaper he found himself wearing. He was glad Sera wasn't around to see *that*.

Or even worse, Riq.

But the diaper was no laughing matter. The more sweat that collected in the suit, the more difficult it was for him to move around. He glanced at the fire inching closer to the control panel. Closer to him.

He needed to get out of the way *now*!

But there was nowhere to run. That was the problem with being in outer space. Well, *one* of the problems.

Fire didn't behave the same on a low-gravity spacecraft. The flames didn't shoot upward in a peak the way they did back home. Up here, they hovered around whatever was burning, a deep blue hue.

"Come on!" Dak shouted as the belt slipped out of his gloved fingers again. A drop of sweat ran into his right eye, momentarily blurring his vision. He blinked away the stinging sensation and looked to his left, where the two other astronauts — who weren't much older than him — were now peering out the window, screaming like little babies. "Uh, little help over here?" Dak shouted.

They didn't even turn around.

He heard a low buzzing sound, barely audible over the screams, but when he looked all around, he couldn't identify the source.

When Dak was finally able to free himself, he drifted awkwardly out of the cockpit, toward the wall with the fire extinguisher. He snatched it in his gloves, removed the safety, and aimed the nozzle at the angry blue flame, which now claimed almost a third of the cockpit. Instead of shooting out straight, though, the white substance oozed out at an upward angle, toward the ceiling. He'd forgotten to take into account the lack of gravity.

Dak adjusted his aim accordingly and drew closer to the fire.

But just as he was starting to gain control of it, the guys near the window started screaming even louder, this time diving toward the center of the cockpit, ignoring the flames, holding on to each other.

Dak dropped the extinguisher and bounded over to the window to see for himself.

And suddenly he was screaming, too.

His eyes were bugging out of his head.

A massive asteroid, more than twice the size of their vessel, was spinning recklessly through space directly toward them. . . .

PART ONE

Looking to the Sky

THE FORCE of the impact slammed Dak against the floor.

He opened his eyes, gasping for breath, expecting to find a hole torn into the ship's main control center, but all he found was a harmless stick lying on the grass next to his face. He stared at the gnarled thing for a few long seconds, trying to wrap his head around where he was — and *when* he was.

He looked up and found his best friend, Sera Froste, standing over him, grinning. A panting dog stood by her side. It looked like it was laughing at him.

"Oops. Sorry," Sera said. But the "sorry" sure sounded sarcastic to Dak.

"What . . . happened?" he asked.

"Errant toss," she said, picking up the stick. "My bad. Nice shoes, by the way."

Dak rubbed the side of his head and sat up, looking at his new pair of checkered Vans as reality slowly crept back into place. He'd been hit by a stick, not an asteroid. And he'd fallen out of his hammock. "Dude," he said, glancing over Sera's shoulder, at his parents' barn—the SMYTH FOR MAYOR signs still scattered throughout the large yard. "I just had the craziest... It was like a Remnant, I think. I was on this space shuttle with these two other astronauts, who were both kind of cowardly, to be honest, and out of the blue comes this asteroid...."

"Yeah, that's not a Remnant, Dak," Sera said. "It's called a dream. Happens when you sleep all day."

Dak was about to argue but lost his train of thought when the mutt began licking the side of his face.

"I think she likes you," Sera said.

"Gross," Dak said, nudging the dog away and climbing to his feet. He wiped the slobber off his cheek and forehead with his shirtsleeve. "What's the deal with the pooch?"

Sera tossed the stick and the dog took off after it. "Long story."

"Oh, I forgot," Dak said, giving her a little sarcasm of his own. "We have *so* many other important places to be right now." He paused for effect. "Not."

Sera rolled her eyes and called for the dog. "Here, Zoe. Here, Bella. Come on, Maxie."

Dak couldn't help but give Sera a hard time. After fixing all the Breaks in history, thus steering the world away from the horrors of the Cataclysm, they'd been safe and sound at home for over a month now. No more history-saving anxiety. No more running from the SQ's thugs or being forced to wear crazy ancient outfits like loincloths or togas. No more warping into dangerous situations, the stress of which had probably taken years off Dak's life of cheese connoisseurship.

In other words, he was bored out of his mind.

Dak and Sera had been arguing for the past two weeks about whether or not to take the Infinity Ring out for a little joyride. All their previous warps had been business trips, Dak argued. Didn't saving the world warrant a "time vacation" or two? Maybe a quick trip back to ancient Hawaii, before anyone had set foot on the islands? Or what about the grand opening of Disneyland in 1955, where they could ride all the rides with the original Mouseketeers? Dak told Sera he'd even consider a more science-oriented trip. Anything to keep him from sleeping away the rest of his days in his parents' itchy hammock.

But Sera believed traveling without a purpose was irresponsible. What if they inadvertently altered some minor detail that set off a chain reaction that changed the world forever — after they'd just spent all this time and effort *fixing* it? She even went so far as hiding the Ring from him.

Before falling asleep, though, Dak had come up with a brand-new argument. And it was perfect. If this one couldn't get Sera to change her mind, nothing could. He just needed to find the right moment to spring it on her.

After all, "timing" was everything. Dak grinned a little at his clever internal wordplay.

"What's so funny?" Sera asked.

"Nothing," Dak told her, wiping the grin off his face. He thought he heard a subtle buzzing sound, like the one he'd heard in his dream, but when he turned toward the barn, he didn't see anything. "Seriously, though," he said, focusing on Sera again, "give me the lowdown on the canine. She looks a little . . . Do you know if she's had her shots?"

Sera gave Dak a dirty look and whistled for the dog to bring back the stick. "Fine," she said. "On my way home from the store yesterday, I found her sitting in the middle of the street, staring up at the clouds like she was in some kind of trance. And then a car came barreling around the corner. I dropped my groceries and sprinted out into the street and tackled her just in time. Both of us went tumbling to the side of the road. I'm not kidding, Dak, that car whizzed right by my nose."

"See?" Dak said, excitedly pointing at her. "It's not so easy to give up being a hero, is it? It's in our blood now, Sera. It's who we are."

"*You* seem to be doing just fine," Sera fired back at him. "Unless your lying around in a hammock somehow benefits humanity."

"Just waiting for my next call to action, Sera."

Sera gave him a little smirk as she pried the stick out of the dog's mouth and gave it another toss, toward

Dak's parents' barn this time, where she had been spending the majority of her free time these days. Dak still wondered why she wasn't spending more time at her place now that she had her parents — even if they *were* sort of weird. Wasn't that all she ever wanted?

Or maybe it was just human nature to take family for granted. Even Dak's own parents, who had seemed so thrilled to have the family back together at first, now spent all their free time campaigning for Dak's mom to become mayor. All he heard around the house was political jargon like *bipartisanship* and *unemployment rate* and *approval ratings*.

"Anyway," Sera said, "now she follows me everywhere I go. Don't you, Fido? Harriet? Stella?"

"I take it she didn't have a tag?" Dak said.

Sera shook her head. "I keep trying out different names, but she doesn't seem to spark to any of them."

"You've just got to find something that reflects her personality. How about Weirdo?" Dak said, realizing this was the most excitement he'd had in weeks. A lost, nameless dog. Possible flea infestation. *Yee-haw!*

"She is pretty strange," Sera said. The dog was now sitting near the barn with the stick in her mouth, staring up at the sky.

"What the heck is she looking at?" Dak asked.

"No idea." Sera put her hands on her hips, still watching the dog. "Every once in a while, she just stops everything and stares into space. Literally. I wonder what's going through her head?"

"Hate to break it to you," Dak said, "but it's not a whole lot. Dogs have brains the size of Hacky Sacks."

When Sera didn't answer, Dak looked into the sky, too, recalling his dream. It had seemed so real. The fire. The asteroid. The slippery seat belt buckle. Even the adult-size diaper. Why would he have a dream about being in space? Did it mean he'd reached a whole new level of adventure withdrawal?

Dak turned back to Sera, deciding now was as good a time as any to roll out his brand-new time-warp argument.

"So," he said, "I've been thinking a lot about Riq."

The Great Disappearance

"WHAT?!" SERA shouted. "I can't *believe* you'd go there, Dak!" She gave him a look of pure fury and started walking toward the barn.

"Wait," Dak said, following behind her. "What'd I say?"

Sera stopped suddenly, causing him to run right into her. "That's a low blow, Dak. Even by *your* standards. Preying on your supposed best friend's emotions just so you can get your way?"

"I just thought—"

"Maybe you should *stop* thinking." Sera planted her hands on her hips. "Because sometimes I wonder if it's *your* brain that's the size of a Hacky Sack."

"—you might wanna check on Riq," Dak said. "We know he'll be in Anatolia in 333 BC, right after Alexander the Great wins the Battle of Issus. My history books say so. Couldn't be simpler. How was I supposed to know you'd blow a gasket?"

Sera reached down to pet the dog while continuing to shoot daggers at Dak. It was understandable for the guy to want to dust off the Ring and warp somewhere for fun. Sera wanted to transport herself back into history somewhere just as badly as Dak. Especially given how things had been going with her parents. But it was risky. And irresponsible. And the fact that Dak would use Riq as a pawn to get her to change her mind . . . that was just wrong.

Riq had sacrificed everything to fix history. He had knowingly uprooted his own family tree for the good of the world and been forced to stay behind in ancient Greece. Treating the Infinity Ring like a toy would be like spitting on his sacrifice.

"Okay, okay," Dak said, running a hand down his face. "Sorry I brought up Riq. It's just . . . in two weeks, school starts back up."

"So?"

Dak cleared his throat. "Sitting in some classroom, surrounded by a bunch of philistines throwing spitballs at one another . . . It doesn't exactly sound like our ideal learning environment. Not when we could be out there in the field, Sera. Reading about history is great, but we could *live* it again."

Sera scoffed. "History almost killed us, if you don't remember. Now, are we done here?"

"For now."

"Good," Sera told him, "because some of us have work to do."

"Ooh," he said, holding out his hands and pretending they were shaking. "More tinkering in my parents' laboratory? I bet it's something *really* important."

Sera was so aggravated now, she wanted to shout again. But she didn't. That would be playing right into his hands. Instead she slapped her hip for her *new* best friend to follow her, and they both set off toward the barn.

"And another thing!" Dak called out behind her. "I'd invest in a pack of flea collars if I was you! Because that new mutt of yours is a straight-up pest factory!"

Sera didn't bother looking back. She and the dog continued inside the barn doors, where she was confronted by her latest scientific failure. It was a petri dish of what was supposed to be tachyon fluid, the most vital ingredient in time travel. When Riq had smashed to pieces the SQ's Eternity Ring in ancient Greece, Sera had seen the green liquid splatter onto his arms and face. She needed to determine its effects on living cells. But so far all she'd done was create some kind of thick green slime that was totally worthless.

Dak didn't know just how close he'd come to winning her over. Of course she wanted to check on Riq. She worried about him constantly.

Then she heard Dak calling to her from outside.

"Sera!" he shouted. "You gotta come see this! There's a pterosaur in the tree above me! I'm not making this up!"

Sera almost burst out laughing.

"Are you listening to this guy, Olive?" she said to the

dog. "A *pterosaur*? Has he officially lost his mind?" She shook her head, trying to imagine how a prehistoric flying reptile played into what was obviously another strategy to get her to dig up the Ring. Dak was getting desperate.

"Sera, hurry! You're not gonna believe this!"

He's got that part right, she thought. *I'm not going to believe it for a second.* "Say hi for me!" she shouted back. Then she took a deep breath and looked at her last empty petri dish. "Am I ever gonna be able to do this?" she said out loud.

She peeked down and found her dog furiously scratching behind her floppy left ear.

What's a Hystorian?

WHEN DAK was about four, he got on a huge dinosaur kick and read every single book about prehistoric life he could get his hands on. It fascinated him to no end that for one hundred thirty-five million years dinosaurs were the dominant terrestrial vertebrates roaming the Earth. What an amazing run, considering humans hadn't even been around for five million years.

That's why Dak's heart was slamming so hard against the inside of his chest now. In the tree above him was a real-life adolescent pterosaur. He was sure of it — even though it was technically impossible. *But just look at that long, toothy jaw,* he told himself. *And that tail. Look at that furry coat* — which he knew was made up of hairlike filaments known as pycnofibers. This wasn't some fake, man-made replica in the Smithsonian. It was the real deal. The pterosaur was young, but Dak could already tell it was going to be huge, which meant it was either a *Quetzalcoatlus* or *Hatzegopteryx*.

Dak caught a whiff of something unpleasant. It wasn't coming from the animal, though. It seemed to be coming from *him*. He looked down at his new Vans, and his heart sank. With his eyes up on the trees, he'd managed to step right in the mess the pterosaur had left behind. He would have been completely grossed out if it wasn't for one simple fact: *He'd just stepped in* dinosaur *poop!*

He quickly caught himself. Technically, referring to the mess on his shoes as *dinosaur poop* was incorrect. What he'd meant to call it was *pterosaur* poop. It was a common mistake to refer to pterosaurs as flying dinosaurs when, in actuality, they were their own separate species.

Dak rubbed his eyes to be sure this wasn't some twisted version of his space dream. But when he looked up, the pterosaur was still sitting in the tree above him, moving its head around. And his shoes still needed a good washing.

What the heck was going on?

Dak turned to call for Sera again, but just then the pterosaur flapped its massive wings and started flying away from him, through the treetops.

He took off after it.

The chase through the forest led Dak clear across town. Occasionally the pterosaur would get way ahead of him and he would assume he'd lost it, but then a hundred yards down the trail he'd find it sitting there in another tree. And it would always look down at him before flying off again, like they were playing some sort of prehistoric game of hide-and-seek.

Dak tried to imagine the conversation he would have with Sera later. "So, what'd you do all day, Dak?" she'd ask him.

"Oh, not much," he'd answer. "Just tailed a pterosaur around the forest for a few hours."

As Dak jogged along the path, he tried to figure out how this was even possible. A real, live prehistoric animal in the forest behind his house. Maybe it was some mutated strain that had lain dormant in a cave for millions of years. Or maybe this was the experiment Sera's parents had been so hush-hush about. They were brilliant, and they were supposed to be working with Dak's parents, but ever since his mom had started campaigning, nobody seemed to have any idea what the Frostes were up to. Cloning prehistoric animals seemed as likely as anything else.

Then another thought occurred to Dak.

What if he and Sera *hadn't* actually fixed all the Breaks in history? What if they'd failed to tie up one or two minor loose ends and over the course of centuries those minor loose ends had become *major* loose ends that had resulted in strange anomalies in the ecosystem, like pterosaurs showing up in the modern world? If that were true, then they'd be forced to warp back into history and fix these loose ends, right? There was no way Sera would be able to argue with *that*.

Dak was so excited, he could hardly breathe—though the breathlessness could've also been the result of ninety straight minutes of continual running.

"Wait for me, pterosaur!" he shouted up at the trees.

And then, eyes fixed on the canopy, he collided with a teenage girl.

They both shrieked on impact and went tumbling to the ground, the girl's books scattering everywhere.

Dak had the wind knocked out of him, but he still managed to glance up at the treetops. His ancient playmate was nowhere to be found.

"What could you *possibly* be in such a hurry about?" the girl shouted, standing up to brush herself off.

Dak opened his mouth to apologize, but quickly realized he knew this girl. It was the young Hystorian who had programmed the SQuare and helped Dak and Sera prepare for their first mission. "Arin!" he shouted. "What a pleasure! Please tell me you saw that pterosaur flying through the forest!"

"Uh, who are you?" Arin said, looking genuinely confused. "And how do you know my name?"

"It's me. Dak." When her face didn't show any sort of recognition, he added, "You helped me and Sera before we warped back in time. And Riq, too. I know you remember Riq. You guys went through, like, Hystorian training together."

"What's a Hystorian?" Arin said, crinkling her nose. "I have no idea what you're talking about. And I'm beginning to think you don't either."

Dak started picking up Arin's books to buy himself a few seconds to think. How could she not know *anything* about the Hystorians? She'd dedicated her entire life to their cause. But he knew the answer. Once they had fixed all the Breaks, they'd also rendered the Hystorian movement unnecessary. Arin didn't know about the Hystorians because the Hystorians no longer existed.

Dak's parents had suggested that he and Sera try to ease back into present-day life. "If you try and dive in too fast," his dad told him, "it'll be overwhelming. Believe me." Hence the hours Dak had been spending in the hammock. But now he understood what his dad meant. The world they'd returned to was different from the one they'd left behind, in both big and small ways.

Case in point, Dak thought as he studied the covers of Arin's books. They weren't the Hystorian guides or science textbooks he expected. They were teen novels about . . . vampires. He handed them back to her, saying, "Did you at least see the pterosaur? It flew right over your head."

Arin studied Dak for a few long seconds. "You're not *seriously* asking me if I saw a flying dinosaur, are you?"

"Well, technically," Dak said, "I asked if you saw a pterosaur. Two totally different prehistoric animals. The one in question existed from the late Triassic period until the end of the Cretaceous period—"

"Okay," Arin interrupted, "you're officially starting to

weird me out." She crinkled her nose again and glanced down at Dak's feet. "Is that ... dog poop?"

Dak looked at his shoes and then back up at Arin. "Actually, it's—"

"If you say it's dinosaur poop, I'm calling 911."

"—pterosaur poop."

Arin set down her books and reached into her bag for her phone.

"It was *there,*" Dak pleaded. "I swear."

"Oh, it all makes sense now," Arin said, typing her pass code into her phone. "Those two farmers who reported seeing UFOs a few days ago ... what they'd actually seen were flying dinosaurs."

"Again, technically—"

"Look," Arin interrupted again. "You seem like a nice enough kid. So I'm not going to call the cops, okay?"

Dak nodded, realizing he wasn't going to convince this version of Arin of anything.

"It's healthy to have a creative imagination," she went on, "but it's probably best if you keep that stuff between you and your little friends, okay? Try finger painting or scrapbooking."

He looked up at the treetops again. "But ..."

"Bye, Dan."

"Dak," he corrected her, but she'd already spun around with her books and started back down the trail.

Dak watched her go, knowing it was a lost cause. She didn't know him at all because in this version of the present, they'd never met. And they'd never met because the Hystorians no longer existed.

What *did* exist, however, was the pterosaur he'd seen flying through the forest. He rubbed his eyes again and looked down at his own palms.

He wasn't dreaming this time.

He was sure of it.

In order to prove it, though, even to himself, he needed to track that animal down.

Bad Science

"FINGERS CROSSED," Sera said to the dog as she added a beaker full of isolated electrons to her latest batch of what she hoped would turn out to be tachyon fluid. She stirred the mix, watching closely through her safety goggles for the slight rise of smoke she knew would signify she was on the right track.

If she had done everything right this time, it would only be a few minutes now.

As Sera stirred, she realized why she'd been so annoyed with Dak. On her way to the barn this morning, she had decided to tell him about the sketch she'd found in her mom's desk drawer a week ago. It looked suspiciously similar to the Infinity Ring . . . or the SQ's Eternity Ring. Underneath the sketch was the beginnings of a formula Sera immediately connected to time travel.

Sera had slammed the drawer closed that day and hurried into her own room and shut the door. What could her parents possibly want with a time-travel device? She had a feeling it wasn't anything good.

After that, Sera began snooping in earnest. She found a large stash of hydrochloric acid in the bathroom medicine cabinet. That was unusual. Acid had a lot of legitimate uses, but it could be harmful if used the wrong way. That was also true of science in general, Sera thought to herself. And her parents were spending a lot of time locked in their lab.

And when they emerged, they were acting downright strange. One night they invited Dak over, and the four of them sat around the table, talking about recent science and history articles and listening to classical music. Everything seemed perfectly normal until her dad had insisted on having an impromptu spitting contest. Even Dak had thought that was weird. He'd run for the hills after the first round.

When Sera returned to her mom's desk drawer the following morning, the sketch and formula were gone.

And so were her parents.

Sera had decided on the walk over to Dak's that a week was long enough. She couldn't keep all this to herself any longer. What good was having a best friend if you couldn't tell him what was bothering you? And her parents' disappearance was definitely bothering Sera. They had worked for Tilda at some point, one of the SQ's most devilish leaders, but they'd never explained why. Or if they'd really had a change of heart. Now Sera couldn't help but assume the worst, that maybe her parents had warped back in time to try to reconnect with the very people she had dedicated her life to fighting.

Too bad Dak turned out to be more concerned with joyriding through history than listening to his best friend.

The dog started whimpering a little, staring out the window of the barn, and Sera reached down to pet her. "At least *you'll* listen to me, right, Lucy? Chloe? Lola?"

Sera remembered that first weekend she was back in the present with her parents. Everything had been so good. They'd started that company with Dak's parents, Solving Quantum Physics. They made the house into a home. They'd even promised to get Sera a puppy. Her parents never came through on that, Sera mused, but she still ended up with a dog. So what if she had a flea or two?

Sera turned back to her latest concoction, but she already knew it was a failure. There definitely would have been signs of smoke by now. And this thick, goopy consistency was all wrong.

She stared at it, baffled.

Normally, she could figure out any science-related conundrum. All it took was a little experimentation, a little tinkering with ingredients. But this tachyon fluid was giving her fits. Maybe she'd lost her confidence. Maybe all that warping through time had done something to her brain.

Then she had another thought. On a whim, she tested the mixture for signs of hydrochloric acid. The results were positive. And a chill settled over Sera as she realized there was only one explanation: sabotage.

Someone had tampered with her equipment.

She threw the entire petri dish into a hazard bag, sealed it up tightly, and took it outside to the trash receptacle. She tossed it on top of at least a dozen other failed attempts and sighed. She almost wished she hadn't figured it out.

When the dog started whimpering again, she knelt down and said, "What is it, girl? Are you frustrated I still haven't guessed your actual name?" The dog barked and Sera realized she wasn't staring up at the sky this time; she was staring at the window. Sera followed the dog's line of vision. What she saw made her gasp.

Hovering just outside the barn's window was a small floating disk. It looked like a miniature UFO built out of pure gold.

"What the . . . ?" Sera stared at it in wonder. When she moved toward it, though, to get a better look, the disk spun around quickly and zipped away.

Sera and the dog both hurried around the other side of the barn and searched all the treetops, but it was gone.

She knew what it was. It was a spy drone.

She'd seen something similar at a tech show she'd attended with Dak a few weeks before their first mission. The man presenting the drone said it was only a model of what a future tracking device might look like. He estimated that it would be another decade before they were ready for actual production.

So what the heck was one doing hovering over Dak's parents' barn, spying on her?

Apology Cheese

DAK DIDN'T waste the next morning lying around in his hammock. He rose early and went straight into the forest to look for his pterosaur. He brought with him a backpack with a half dozen skyrockets. The plan was to fire them off in the middle of the forest in hopes that the pterosaur would be drawn to the loud, crackling sound and bright lights.

Unless he was losing his mind, that is.

Dak had to admit, there was a little bit of doubt knocking around in the back of his head. Was he *positive* what he'd seen was an actual pterosaur? It's not like he'd gotten close enough to touch its skin or look into its eyes. What if it was only a robotic replica some tech wizard had created in order to scare kids walking through the forest?

But that wouldn't explain the poop.

The only other explanation Dak could think of was human error. *His* human error. What if all that warping around had altered his brain chemistry to the point that he was no longer able to differentiate between dream and reality? He recalled the look on Arin's face when he'd mentioned the pterosaur. She thought he was crazy. Then again, she also thought he was crazy for mentioning the Hystorians.

After hiking around the forest for several hours, with no sign of the pterosaur, Dak lit his fourth skyrocket. He watched it arc above the trees, into the sky, where it exploded into a glittery mass of colors. Dak had always loved fireworks, but this was different. This was a "pterosaur call."

He stood there for a good ten, fifteen minutes.

Waiting.

But his prehistoric pal never showed up.

Dak stepped off the trail to rest on a fallen tree trunk. He'd never felt so alone. Arin had no clue who he was, Riq was exiled in ancient history, his parents spent all their time campaigning, and now, he was fighting with Sera.

Just then, as if he'd summoned her somehow, Sera emerged from the bushes. She had leaves in her hair, and she was wearing a backpack he'd never seen before. "*There* you are," she said, slightly out of breath.

"Uh, what are you doing in the middle of the forest?" he asked, making room for her on the tree trunk. He heard the same buzzing sound he'd heard the day before, near the barn, but this time it seemed to be coming from Sera herself.

That's weird, he thought. He definitely needed to get his head checked.

"I was looking for *you,*" she said, plopping down next to him. "I followed the fireworks."

Dak watched Sera reach into her backpack and pull out a brown paper bag. She held it out to him, saying, "Snack?"

He unfolded the bag and looked inside. It held a beautiful hunk of his current favorite cheese: aged Gouda. He looked up at Sera skeptically. "What's *this* for?"

"What, I can't bring my best friend a tasty treat?" she asked.

"Of course you can," Dak told her. "In fact, I encourage it. But . . ."

"What?"

"It just seems a little out of the blue," Dak said. "Considering you almost bit my head off yesterday."

"Oh, right," Sera said, her eyes dropping. "That's actually the reason I was looking for you. Listen, I overreacted, Dak. I'm sorry."

"You are?" Dak was more confused by Sera's apology than his imaginary pterosaur sighting. In all the years he'd known her, she'd told him she was sorry exactly twice.

"Not only that," Sera went on. "I've been hiding something from you, Dak. Something really important."

That clinched it. There was definitely something strange going on with Sera. But he had a feeling he knew what it was. "Look, Sera," he said, "if something's going on with your parents, you can talk to me anytime. Seriously, my door's always open. You know that, right?"

"What?" Sera said. A grin slowly came over her face, and she let out a laugh. "No, Dak. My parents are perfectly fine. Overworked, maybe, but all that matters to me is that we're together."

Dak stared at Sera like she had two heads. "Uh, okay," he said. "Then what's going on?"

"I didn't want to say anything until I was one hundred percent sure it was going to work." Sera looked over her shoulder and scooted closer. "I put the SQuare back together, Dak."

"You did?" Dak said. "I thought you said it was destroyed beyond repair."

"Yeah, well, I thought so." Sera looked a little less certain now. "But I'm that good. Anyway, you're not gonna believe what it said."

"What?" Dak's heart started beating faster.

Sera cleared her throat. "We missed one. We missed a Break. And it's the most important Break of all."

Dak's eyes grew wide with excitement. "No way!" he shouted, leaping off the tree trunk. Butterflies flapped around in his stomach. Finally, some real action. "Where? When?"

"Ninth-century China," Sera said, standing up. "Something went very wrong during that time period, and we have to go fix it."

Dak wrapped Sera in a bear hug, lifted her in the air, and twirled her around, shouting, "Yes! Yes! I knew there was more for us to do!"

"Dak, please, let me down."

"My bad," he said, dropping her on her feet. He watched Sera pull the beautiful Infinity Ring out of her backpack. "Why's it gold now?" he asked her.

"It's new and improved," she told him. "I thought it was time for an upgrade. Now all that's left to do is program the coordinates."

"Wait," Dak said, feeling unexpectedly anxious. This was all he wanted, right? So why was he so hesitant? He cleared his throat and said, "Shouldn't we, like, tell our parents first?"

Sera punched in the coordinates, saying, "I already left a note in both our houses."

"Wow, great," Dak said, nodding. Sera had certainly covered all the bases. All he had to worry about was fixing history again. "So, I take it your parents agreed to watch the flea sack, then."

"The what?" Sera looked up at him, confused.

"Your rescue dog," Dak said. "I just wondered who was going to feed that bag of germs while you were gone."

"Oh. Right. The dog." Sera looked up and down the

trail again. "Trust me, he's way safer here. My mom will take care of him."

Dak nodded. "Cool."

"Grab on," Sera said, holding out the golden Ring.

Dak gripped one side of the thing as Sera slung her bag over her shoulder. Before she pushed the ACTIVATE button, she looked up at Dak and said, "Ready?"

"Ready." Dak searched the treetops one last time for his pterosaur, but it was still nowhere to be found.

When he turned back to Sera, he found her staring at him with a concerned look on her face. "What is it?" he said, not wanting anything to keep them from their mission.

"Is there something wrong with the cheese I got you?" she asked. "You haven't even touched it."

Dak looked down at his hunk of Gouda, still perfectly intact. Only time travel could possibly distract him from eating a piece of high-end cheese. "No, it's outstanding," he assured Sera. To prove it, he took a huge bite and smiled as he chewed.

"That's more like it," Sera said, her face lit up with approval. "Okay, here we go."

Dak watched her push the ACTIVATE button.

The Ring glowed and shook in Dak's hand. He barely had time to take a second bite of cheese before the sweet weightlessness of time travel spread through his entire being.

PART TWO

6

The Tang Dynasty

DAK WOKE up on a cot in a small bamboo hut, with a familiar buzzing sound in his ears. He sat up, still half dazed, and looked around. Sera was there, shoving what looked like modern medical supplies into her small leather knapsack. She was wearing a not-so-modern-looking brown cap on her head, strange-looking riding pants, and a white blouse. And there was a small robotic disk hovering in the air near her head.

Dak rubbed his eyes and looked at the disk again, trying to decide if they'd warped into ancient China or the set of some science fiction movie.

"Where are we?" Dak said, stretching out his arms and neck. He pointed at the flying disk. "And what the heck is *that* thing?"

"Oh, you're up," Sera said, emotionless. "There's a traditional robe on the bench for you, next to your back-pack. But please stay in the hut until I get back."

"What's wrong?" he asked.

She looked up at Dak and gave a fake smile.

"Everything's going according to plan," she said. "I just have something kind of important to do right now."

Dak slid off the bed. "Was I, like, asleep for a long time or something?" He was usually so excited to be in another time period, he couldn't sleep at all.

"You were asleep for over a day," Sera said, closing her knapsack. "But don't worry, I picked up the slack like usual. I found some local clothes for us to wear, and I made sure there were no Time Wardens. And just this morning, I learned where to find the local expert in *waidan*."

"*Waidan*?" Dak said, allowing the word to bang around his bleary brain for a few seconds. "Isn't that the ancient Chinese version of alchemy?"

"Wow," Sera said. "You really do know a lot. But I've got this one covered. You, Dak, are going to sit here and rest your tired little head. I left some more of that cheese you like on the counter. Eat up and I'm sure you'll get your strength back."

Dak saw another hunk of Gouda on the counter, and his stomach instantly grumbled. If he'd been asleep for a full day, it also meant he hadn't eaten in a full day. Cheese would be the perfect remedy. "But I don't understand," he said, turning back to Sera. "I've *never* fallen asleep during a warp."

"You probably had a bug or something," Sera said, moving toward the door. "Seriously, rest up. I don't mind taking the lead on this one."

How strange, Dak thought. He didn't *feel* sick. Not at all. In fact, other than the hunger pangs, he felt great. So why couldn't he remember anything beyond the moment he put his hand on the Infinity Ring?

"Wait," Dak called to Sera as she started opening the door. He moved toward the wooden bench. "Just let me throw on this ridiculous-looking robe and I'll join you."

"No!" Sera barked.

Dak froze. "What? Why not?" She'd never spoken to him like that before.

Sera's face softened. "I mean . . . I'm late as it is, Dak. Just relax, okay? I need you in top form for the next warp."

"What next warp?"

"I'll explain later," she said. "But trust me, you'll enjoy our next destination *way* more than boring ninth-century China."

Dak let the robe fall back onto the bench. "Boring ancient China?" he said, outraged. "I'm *fascinated* by ancient China, Sera. You know that. Remember when I spent an entire weekend reading the Song Dynasty treatise *Wujing Zongyao*? And I'm still in awe about the four great inventions of the Chinese culture. You remember what they are, right?"

"Dak, I really —"

"The compass, gunpowder, papermaking, and printing," Dak told her. "Four staples of modern life. How could anyone think ancient China was boring?"

"Okay, okay, I get it," Sera said. "You like China.

Just . . . be a good boy and eat your cheese. I'll be back."

"At least tell me what *this* thing's all about." The hovering disk seemed to be looking back and forth between Dak and Sera.

"That's ABe," Sera said, cracking a genuine smile this time. "My pet smart-drone."

"Where'd you get a smart-drone?"

"You know all that time I was spending in your parents' barn?" Sera made a clicking sound with her tongue, and the mechanical disk whipped around the small room and then perched on her shoulder. "I was building the world's first mechanical pet." She then snapped her fingers and held open her knapsack, and "ABe" buzzed right inside and powered itself off.

"Whoa," Dak said. "Definitely beats that fleabag you were hanging around the other day. But I thought you said you were putting together the SQuare while you were in the barn."

"This *is* the SQuare, Dak," Sera said. "That's what makes the smart-drone so smart. Now, rest up." She pushed through the small bamboo door and let it swing closed behind her.

"Wait!" Dak called out, hurrying to the door and poking his head out into the bright, sunny day. "Where *are* we exactly? And what Break are we trying to fix? You never even told me."

Sera stopped near the far end of a large, empty courtyard. "We're in the capital city of Chang'an," she said. "During the heyday of the Tang Dynasty."

"Okay, and . . . ?"

"*You're* the one who's supposed to be the history buff," Sera told him. "Go eat your cheese. I promise I'll be back soon." And with that, she disappeared out of the courtyard.

Dak studied the well-groomed trees that lined the perimeter of the courtyard, trying to figure out what had gotten into Sera. Was she really that mad that he'd slept through an entire day? It's not like he *wanted* to sleep that long. He was sick. She even said so herself. Though he definitely didn't feel sick now. Groggy, maybe, but not sick.

A sad thought then occurred to Dak as he sulked back in the dark hut. What if Sera wished Riq were on the warp with her, instead of him? Did she think Riq was a more useful history-fixing road dog?

Dak glanced at the cheese she'd left for him. It looked quite exquisite, he had to admit. And he was definitely hungry. But he didn't have time to eat. No, he had to get out there and prove himself to Sera. He'd show her who was the better Hystorian.

Dak turned his back on the cheese and made a bee-line for the robe.

7

The Legume Thief

THE MOMENT he heard voices, Dak ducked out of sight behind a large manicured bush. He had a clear view of a nearby courtyard, where a group of men dressed in fancy golden robes seemed to be interrogating a boy no older than he was. The men took turns shouting things at the boy and pointing their fingers at him, but Dak couldn't understand a word they were saying. Warping back in time and across the planet was a little more difficult, he realized, when you didn't have a translation device.

One of the men pointed to the dirt floor of the courtyard at a sack, which was overflowing with what looked to be legumes. Based on how thin the boy was and the poor quality of his clothing, Dak wondered if he'd stolen from the men. Still, he wished he could do something to help. The boy looked like he needed the nourishment much more than the men surrounding him.

Dak decided it was best to leave things alone, though.

This dispute wasn't any of his business. And he needed to continue looking for Sera.

He still had no idea what Break they were supposed to be fixing or why they needed to fix it, but if he could find an alchemist, he figured he'd find Sera, too, and she'd explain everything. Leaving him in the hut was a test. She wanted to make sure he was still committed to the Hystorian cause and not just some lazy scrub who was addicted to hammocks.

But Dak was quickly realizing how hard it would be to gather information in an ancient city when nobody understood a word he was saying. Sure, he could list tons of facts about the Tang Dynasty. Like, he knew it was founded by the Li family, who seized power after the collapse of the Sui Empire. And he knew Chang'an, the city Sera said they were in, was currently the most populated city in the world. But all the historical info at his disposal couldn't make up for the fact that he was lost without Riq's translation device. Or without Riq himself.

Maybe Riq really was more valuable on these warps than Dak. At the very least, Riq had always managed to stay awake.

Dak sighed. He was just about to leave when one of the men suddenly wound up and slugged the boy right in the gut.

Hard.

Dak cringed just watching it.

He didn't know what to do. He couldn't just leave

the young thief here to fend for himself. On the other hand, there were five golden-robed men and only one Dak. And these guys seemed nasty. What was he going to do, challenge them to a fistfight?

One of them stepped up to the boy and boxed his ears.

The boy let out a yelp.

Dak remembered the two remaining skyrockets in his backpack. And the matches. He knew how consumed the Chinese would eventually become with fireworks — which they would use at first to ward off evil spirits. What if Dak introduced fireworks a few decades ahead of schedule?

A third man stepped up to the boy and slugged him in the stomach again. The boy doubled over and coughed up a little blood this time. The men laughed.

Dak had to act *now*.

He took out the first skyrocket, planted the tail in the dirt in plain view of the men, and got his match ready. "Hey!" he shouted.

The five men looked up at Dak, their faces full of confusion . . . and then rage. One of them shouted something Dak couldn't understand.

"You guys want to see something crazy?" he shouted back. He knew they had no idea what he was saying, but it didn't matter. His words weren't the important part. Dak pointed at the bright blue sky and said, "Watch me light up the heavens before your very eyes."

Two of the men began marching toward Dak, and they didn't look like they were coming in peace.

Dak quickly lit the match and put his flame under the fuse. He watched it start chewing its way up to the explosive. Just as the two men grabbed Dak by his elbows, there was a loud blast and the skyrocket launched into the sky above the courtyard, exploding into an array of sparkling colors.

The robed men all stared up at the sky in awe. The two who held Dak released him. One of them even bowed dramatically at his feet.

"You like that?" Dak said, grinning. "I have one more if you want it."

They responded in a language Dak couldn't understand, of course, so he dusted off his nonverbal communication skills. He held up the final firework and mimed planting it into the ground. Then he showed them how to strike a match and pretended to light the fuse.

All five men were near him now, nodding their heads and speaking in their native tongue. As diversions went, this one had been a big win. But Dak noticed that the boy still hadn't run away. His feet, Dak then realized, were tied together with rope.

Dak put the skyrocket and matches on the ground and backed away, motioning for the men to try it themselves. When they converged on the firework, Dak hurried over to the boy and dropped to his knees to untie the rope. By the time one of the men turned around, Dak had freed the boy. He handed him the sack of legumes and shoved him toward the exit.

The man took a step toward Dak and the boy, but they were already in a full sprint out of the courtyard. Dak led the boy down a dirt road, through a row of seller stalls and crowds of merchants and people milling around, many of them still looking up at the sky even though the colors had long since fizzled away.

Dak turned around, expecting to see the men chasing after them, but there was nobody.

He slowed to a stop about a hundred yards down the path and stood there sucking in breath. He looked behind them again. Still nobody. Then he turned to the boy and said, "Go on, dude, get out of here. You're a free man."

The boy just stood there, though, not understanding a word Dak was saying.

Dak pointed at the dirt path ahead of them. "Take your legumes and go." He even pulled the hunk of Gouda out of his bag and handed it to the boy. "And take this. You need it more than I do."

The boy stared down at the cheese, baffled.

"You eat it," Dak said. "Like this." He pretended to stuff something into his mouth and fake-chewed.

The boy seemed to understand because he took a bite of the cheese, his eyes immediately lighting up with pleasure. He had a dark birthmark on his cheek that looked like a crescent moon. For some reason, it reminded Dak of his dream about being in space, and the fire, and the asteroid coming right at him. It had been so vivid. If he didn't know better, he really would think he'd had a Remnant. Or maybe it was a premonition. Was that even possible?

"It's called Gouda," Dak told the boy. "And it's about twenty times more valuable than that firework back—"

Dak was interrupted by a blast in the distance. He looked up and watched the skyrocket soar above the city, bursting into an array of beautiful colors. All of the people nearby were pointing up at the sky, oohing and aahing. Some started toward the courtyard to see where all the color was coming from.

The boy swallowed another bite of cheese and tried to hand Dak the sack of legumes. Dak shook his head, a thought suddenly occurring to him. The boy didn't understand a word of English, but Dak knew at least one word in the local dialect. "*Waidan*," he said.

"*Waidan*?" the boy repeated.

"Yes," Dak said. "*Waidan*. Where"—he put a flattened hand over his eyebrows, like a military salute, and pretended to be looking all around—"can I find some alchemy?"

"*Waidan*," the boy excitedly repeated three more times. And then he began pulling Dak down the street.

8

The Evils of Gunpowder

THE CHINESE boy with the birthmark led Dak to a dark, wooden warehouse shoved right up against a Buddhist monastery. Dak had read about these early monasteries, but seeing one in person was astonishing. It was beautifully landscaped with flowers everywhere, and several monks were walking in silence along a cobblestone path, heads bowed.

Dak felt like he should be tiptoeing out of respect.

The boy unlatched a thick wooden door and led Dak inside, where it was extremely dark and damp. They had to pass through a long, narrow hall lit up by a few dull torches. When they came upon an open door, the boy pointed inside and said in a quiet voice, "*Waidan.*"

"Thank you," Dak told him, bowing slightly. He didn't know where the bow had come from but it felt right, especially after seeing the monastery. Dak expected the boy to spin around and hurry his sack of legumes and

Gouda back home to his family, but he just stood there behind Dak, nodding.

Dak shrugged and ducked his head inside the door.

He spotted Sera immediately. She was standing next to an older Chinese man, who had to be the alchemist. His dark workroom was set up like an ancient version of Dak's parents' barn. There were dozens of stone bowls filled with powders and plant clippings, and a faint smell of sulfur hung over the room.

Sera and the ancient alchemist were both leaning over an old wooden table, and the man seemed to be explaining something in his ancient Chinese tongue. Sera was nodding, which meant she had to be wearing a translation device. Dak wondered where she got it and why he didn't have one, too.

The man then added a chemical to one of the small stone bowls, which resulted in a minor explosion that made both of them leap back from the workbench.

"*Waidan*," the boy whispered over Dak's shoulder. His breath smelled like Gouda, which Dak found surprisingly pleasant.

"Yeah, I kind of gathered that," Dak whispered back.

All the pieces finally came together in Dak's mind. Fireworks. Ninth-century China. An anonymous alchemist toiling away in a dark room. Dak had just witnessed history. This man had just discovered the chemical recipe for gunpowder!

Dak was about to step into the room and congratulate

the man when Sera did something he never would have expected. He gasped in disbelief as she took a syringe out of her knapsack and jabbed the long needle into the old man's neck.

Sera caught the alchemist as he collapsed and lay him gently on his back. Then she stood up in front of the workbench and started collecting all the man's stored chemicals, shoving them into her knapsack.

Dak stepped out from behind the door, shouting, "What are you doing?"

"Dak!" Sera said, startled. "What are *you* doing? I told you to wait for me in the hut."

"I came looking for you," Dak barked.

The boy raced past Dak to get inside. He pushed Sera away, and held up the old man's head and started speaking to him in a quiet voice.

Dak marched over to Sera and pointed at the syringe in her hand. "What'd you do, kill him?"

"No, I didn't *kill* him," Sera said. "It's a perfectly safe chemical blend that will put our friend to sleep for several hours. When he wakes up, he won't remember anything about the dangerous elements he was experimenting with."

Dak looked down at the man, trying to understand what was happening. Things seemed to be spiraling out of control, and he didn't know what to do. "Why are we here, Sera?" he finally demanded. "What's the Break we're fixing? I need to know *now.*"

Sera sighed, shoving the syringe back into her knapsack. "Fine, here's the situation, Dak. Remember back home, near your barn, when you said you wanted to go back into history again?"

Dak nodded.

"It got me thinking about what a great opportunity we had. Instead of just fixing Breaks this time, we could actually make life better for people."

"Funny," Dak said. "I wouldn't think that involved stabbing old people in the neck."

"Look," Sera said. "We can't do it all the time because, you know, every little change we make creates massive ripple effects throughout time. Which is incredibly dangerous. Blah, blah, blah. But I decided maybe we can alter a few key moments in time for the better. Do you know what this man was doing in here?"

"Of course," Dak said. "He was inventing gunpowder."

"That's right." Sera grabbed Dak by his shoulders and stared right into his eyes. "And do you realize how much death and destruction the invention of gunpowder ultimately leads to? Think about it, Dak. Guns, explosives, war, horrific acts of terrorism. And we have the opportunity to stop it all right now. Today, Dak. Me and you."

Sera had a point. The invention of gunpowder would lead, directly and indirectly, to a ton of horrible historical events. But he still didn't see how putting one man to sleep in some dank, ancient Chinese warehouse was going to stop *anything*.

Sera gestured at Dak's shoes. "You stick out like a sore thumb with those checkered Vans, by the way."

Dak glanced at his shoes, then cleared his throat and said, "Someone's going to figure out the formula eventually, Sera."

"Of course they will," she fired back. "But our responsibility is to make sure the inventor is someone more trustworthy, someone who will aim to use this advancement for the greater good. In this case, actually, it's a *group* of people."

"But how do we know—"

"Come on," Sera said, cutting him off. "We have to hurry up and get these chemicals into the hands of the ancient pacifist group known as the AB."

"The AB?" Dak said, more confused than ever. "Who the heck is the AB?"

"Just follow me," Sera said.

Dak looked down at the alchemist again, the man he'd been searching for all morning. He was shocked to find the boy with the moon-shaped birthmark asleep on the dirt beside the old man. Dak reached down and tried to wake up the little thief by jostling his arm, but the poor kid was out cold. He was even snoring a little. All the excitement of the day must have finally caught up with him.

"Dak, let's go," Sera said, tugging at his elbow. "We don't have time to mess around."

As they left the warehouse, Dak found the sack of

legumes next to the door. He ran it back inside and lay it next to the boy so he'd have something to eat when he woke up. Before he turned to leave, he saw that the boy was still clutching a small piece of Gouda in his right hand. He'd eaten almost all of it.

Dak shook the kid again.

Nothing.

He stared at the remaining Gouda again, thinking about how he'd slept through an entire day. And he remembered the cheese was the last thing he'd eaten before nodding off.

"Are you coming?" Sera called to him from the door.

Dak spun around and looked his best friend up and down. He nodded, climbing to his feet. He followed her back through the hall, pretending like everything was perfectly fine when really everything was perfectly messed up. Had Sera given him a bad piece of cheese?

Had she known it was going to make him fall asleep?

It hurt his chest to think that his best friend in the world might be involved in some dubious mission that she was keeping from him. But she had outright lied about there being another Break. What else might she be hiding?

The AB Pacifists

THEY WOUND through the narrow streets of the city until they came upon a familiar-looking courtyard, where Dak stopped in his tracks. This was the exact same courtyard where he'd freed the birthmark boy.

Which meant . . .

Sera stopped, too, and turned around to face him. "What *now*, Dak?" she said, rolling her eyes at him. ABe, her pet flying robot, buzzed just overhead.

"Uh, you go on ahead," he said. "I'll be, like, the lookout man or whatever. I'll make sure no one tries to mess up the exchange."

"Fine," Sera said, shrugging. She held open her knapsack. "ABe, power off." The robotic disk slipped itself inside, went dark, and Sera continued into the courtyard.

Dak snuck right up to the entrance and hid behind the same bush he'd hidden behind only a few hours earlier, when he had stopped to watch the men in golden robes interrogate the legume thief.

His stomach sank as he watched Sera approach those same men now. They were smiling and waving at her, like they were all old friends. How was this possible? What exactly had he missed while he was out cold in that hut? If Sera knew these men had just roughed up a starving boy, she wouldn't be acting all buddy-buddy with them.

Or would she?

Dak had no idea what to do or think. It was like his best friend had become a completely different person overnight.

Dak shook his head and tried putting those thoughts out of his head. From his hiding place, he watched Sera lay out the chemicals on a table in front of the men and start speaking to them in the local dialect. He assumed she was explaining how to make gunpowder.

Sure enough, in a few minutes, her concoction produced a minor explosion, just like the one the old man had created in the warehouse. The golden-robed men all took a step back and smiled from ear to ear, and nodded and shook hands.

Great, Dak thought. *These guys won't just be using their fists the next time they torture some kid who tries to swipe a few veggies. They'll be using explosives, too.*

How was this helping people live better lives?

Sera bid the men good-bye and hurried back across the courtyard. She squatted down near Dak, pulled ABe out of her knapsack, and started using it like a tablet now. Dak saw that it was a shiny gold on top, with a full keypad. "Okay," she said, her fingers flying across the keys. "Let me just look up the coordinates and we'll move on to the next place."

"Where'd you get that?" Dak asked her.

"ABe?" she said. "I already told you. While you were asleep in your hammock—"

"Let me guess," Dak said, interrupting her, "you were in the barn creating a flying drone that doubled as a SQuare, and you made it gold for some reason. And you did all this while simultaneously redesigning the Infinity Ring."

"Actually, you have it about right," Sera said. A snarky grin came over her face and she added, "You're finally beginning to catch on, Dacky Boy."

Dacky Boy?

Sera had never once called him Dacky Boy in all the years he'd known her. He stared into this girl's eyes, searching for Sera. *His* Sera. The one he'd grown up with and traveled back in time with and fought the SQ with.

But she wasn't there.

This Sera was cocky and secretive, and she called him stupid nicknames. The only explanation he could come up with was that she was hurting. Maybe the reunion with her parents had changed her somehow. If so, it was up to him to figure out how to help her.

Sera pulled out the golden Infinity Ring and placed it next to the golden drone.

Dak glanced around the hedge and saw the men playing with the chemicals Sera had just given them. Men in gold robes.

Strange, he thought.

"So, where to now?" Dak asked, trying to sound casual.

Sera was busy punching coordinates into the Ring. "Massachusetts," she said without looking up.

"America?" Dak said, surprised. "What year?"

"You'll see," she said, looking up at him. "But I'm pretty sure you'll feel right at home at Aunt Effie's farm. I heard her barn even has a hammock."

"Sweet," Dak said, playing along.

But in his head, he was repeating, again and again, the name of the farm she'd just mentioned.

Aunt Effie's farm.

Aunt Effie's farm.

Why did that sound so familiar?

Sera stood up, slipping the drone back into her knapsack. "Did you eat the cheese I left for you in the hut?" she asked.

Dak nodded, his knees suddenly going weak.

"That's odd," she said, studying him. She reached back into her knapsack and pulled out a smaller chunk of Gouda, handing it to Dak. "You better eat this, too. I can't have you getting sick on me again."

"Oh, awesome," Dak deadpanned. "I was just starting to feel hungry, too." He took the cheese and took a big bite while she watched him. He left the chunk under his tongue, though, as he pretended to be chewing.

There was no way he was eating anything else she gave him. Not until he figured out what she was up to.

There was a small explosion from the courtyard, and when Sera turned around to look, Dak spit the cheese out into his hand and chucked it into the bushes. He did the same with the rest of the cheese.

When she turned back around, Dak fake-swallowed and wiped his mouth, saying, "Wow, that Gouda was seriously gourmet, but I sure am feeling tired. Don't worry, though, Sera. I'll do my best to stay awake so I can help you on the next warp."

Sera grinned. "I know you will, Dak. You're so committed to the cause." She punched a few more buttons on the Ring and told him, "Okay, hang on."

Dak took hold of the Ring as Sera hit the ACTIVATE button. The thing lit up in his grasp, and the world around him began to swirl again, and as Dak was pulled into the abyss this time, he suddenly realized the significance of Aunt Effie's farm in Massachusetts. It was the site of physicist Robert Goddard's most notable invention — the first liquid-fuel rocket.

But just as Dak started trying to understand the connection between gunpowder and rockets, he was lost to the darkness.

1 0

The Rocket Launch

DAK STOOD in the middle of a snow-covered field, shivering and staring at what he believed to be the launching frame of the world's first liquid-fuel rocket. It was freezing cold, and he was still shaken up about his time in ancient China, but none of that could stop him from grinning ear to ear. If this contraption was what he thought it was, he knew this day would go down in history. And he was here to witness it firsthand.

Unless he was mistaken.

Dak wanted to confirm with Sera, who was the one who had punched in all the coordinates, but that was impossible at the moment. Sera was still sitting in the snow, rubbing her temples, totally out of it. This particular warp had been especially hard on her for some reason.

"Sera?" Dak said in a tentative voice.

He placed his hand on her shoulder and gave it a gentle shake.

Nothing.

Regardless of what he'd seen Sera do in China, he had decided to give her the benefit of the doubt. This was his best friend in the world, after all. He had to trust that there was a method to her madness. Whatever mistakes she'd made, it was up to *him* to bring her back to the righteous side.

"Sera?" Dak said again.

When she didn't answer this time, he took a few steps toward the rocket. He wrapped his arms around himself to fight against the bitter cold. His teeth chattered. But none of that mattered right now. He had to get a better look at the contraption in the distance. The rocket itself was thin, and he was still standing a good fifty yards away, but he was sure it was the early work of physicist Robert Goddard. He could tell because the engine was built into the top of the rocket, and Dr. Goddard would only later discover it was better to have the engine positioned near the bottom of the rocket.

Butterflies spread through Dak's stomach.

If he was correct in his assumption and what Sera had said before the warp was true, then the date was March 16, 1926, and they were on Aunt Effie's farm in Auburn, Massachusetts. This date was historic because Dr. Goddard's liquid-fuel rocket would rise forty-one feet in the air, and it would remain in flight for 2.5 seconds. Those numbers might not sound all that impressive, but Dak knew they would change the course of history forever.

"You're awake?" Sera said, startling Dak.

She walked up behind him, opening up her knapsack. Dak watched her small, robotic disk power on and fly around her head a few times before settling on her shoulder.

"Why wouldn't I be awake?" Dak asked. His question was a test. He was giving her the benefit of the doubt, yes, but he wasn't a dummy. He knew it was possible — and even likely — that she had drugged him on purpose. But he still needed to figure out why.

"No reason," Sera said, staring across the field at the rocket. "I'm just, um, glad you're feeling better."

Dak and Sera both watched a group of people dressed in warm coats step out of the farmhouse and begin trudging through the snow, toward the rocket. He quickly forgot about testing Sera because this was it. Dr. Goddard was about to initiate his history-changing launch.

Sera took Dak by the arm and pulled him out of sight behind a thick, snow-covered tree.

When she let go of his arm, Dak said, "I can't believe we're about to see the first liquid-fuel rocket take flight, Sera. This is a huge moment in global history. That's physicist Robert H. Goddard and his crew chief, Henry Sachs, and —"

"Quiet," Sera barked at him. "ABe, I need the details of our whereabouts. Volume level one, please."

To Dak's amazement, Sera's robotic disk lit up and made a series of buzzing sounds. "Today is March 16,

1926," it stated in a quiet, computerized voice. "You are in Auburn, Massachusetts. Across the snow-filled farm, you should see Professor Robert Goddard walking alongside his crew chief, Henry Sachs. Just behind them are Esther Goddard and Percy Roope."

"Whoa," Dak said. "It's like a flying, talking SQuare. You really made that in my parents' barn?"

Sera shrugged.

Dak wanted to tell Sera that there was nothing her little pet microchip could tell her that he couldn't. And he was more than a little offended that she would shush him in favor of a tin can.

Dak looked at Sera's profile. It was the real her on the outside, all right, but it certainly wasn't her on the inside. And for the first time since running into her in the forest, he wondered if he was actually in danger.

"Sera," he said, "I need you to tell me what we're doing here. Please."

"I don't know if you've noticed," she answered, pulling a syringe out of her knapsack, "but I'm a little busy at the moment." She pushed the needle into a small vial, sucked up all the liquid medicine inside, and then held it up to her eye level as she squirted out a few drops.

Dak's heart sped up at the sight of the needle. "Is that what you used on the alchemist?"

"How very perceptive of you," Sera answered in an especially snarky voice.

Dak took her by the arm. "Sera," he said, stern but

gentle. "What's going on with you? Seriously."

Sera looked at Dak's hand on her elbow and then looked up at him. "Everything's fine," she said, ripping her elbow free. "Strike that. It's *more* than fine. I feel like I'm finally able to do the work I always dreamed of doing when we were hopping all up and down the time stream, doing whatever the Hystorians told us to do. We're no longer just fixing history, Dak. We're improving people's lives."

"You're not really acting like yourself, though," Dak countered. "I *know* you."

"Okay, okay," Sera said, taking a deep breath and blowing it out slowly. "You're right, Dak. You've always been able to pick up on my moods."

"Exactly," Dak said, feeling like he was finally getting through to her.

"I'm a little stressed," she said. "I want so badly for the world to be a better place." She paused and looked up into the sky, and to Dak's surprise, a single tear spilled out of her left eye and ran down her cheek. She wiped it away and looked at him.

He saw her in that second.

His Sera.

"I just need you to understand what it looks like from my perspective," Dak told her. "You're putting people to sleep with a needle and walking around with a robotic Frisbee on your shoulder. But whatever, Sera. I believe in you. I just want you to let me in on the plan."

Sera took a few more deep breaths, nodding. "You're right, Dak. You really are. I've been so caught up in wanting to do good, I've failed to include my . . . you know . . . best friend."

Dak nodded. "Exactly. You know how helpful I am. I don't mean to brag but I'm *way* more useful than Riq. You just have to give me a chance."

Sera motioned around the tree. "This man, Dak—"

"Robert Goddard," he said.

"Yes." Sera peeked her head around the tree at the group of people gathered around the rocket. "By coming up with the first liquid-fuel rocket—"

"Three minutes until launch," the flying can opener said. "The Pacifists will be coming out of the house in two minutes and thirty-five seconds."

The Pacifists? Dak remembered the golden-robed men in China. Could the computer be talking about the same people? Did they have a time-travel device, too? And who were they anyway? A "pacifist" was a person who didn't believe in violence, but that hardly described those brutal men.

"By coming up with the first liquid-fuel rocket," Sera went on, "Dr. Goddard is paving the way for a number of terrible inventions. Think about it, Dak. Missiles, atomic bombs, even nuclear weapons. These are all things that threaten the well-being of everyone on the planet."

Dak watched Sera prepare a second needle. Her knapsack was lying by her feet, and he saw the tip of the golden Infinity Ring peeking out. "When you said you wanted to help people," he said, "I was thinking much more specifically. Like, imagine if we were able to stop Adolf Hitler from ever gaining power in Germany. Think about how much good *that* would do. The things we're doing now are too general, aren't they?"

"Not in my opinion."

"Think about it," Dak said. "Stopping the invention of gunpowder? Stopping rocket technology? These advancements are inevitable, Sera. I don't see how this is helping anyone."

Sera sighed and glanced up into the sky again. "The universe is so enormous, isn't it?" she asked.

"Uh, I guess so," Dak said. He had no idea what this had to do with anything they were talking about. Was she referring to the dream he'd told her about?

"One minute," the flying SQuare said.

"Have you ever looked up at the moon and wondered what it would be like if all of humankind started fresh?" Sera looked at Dak. "Maybe we've messed it all up down here. Maybe it's too late."

When Dak looked into the sky, all he could think about was his dream. He felt nauseated remembering how he was trapped in the seat belt. The fire inching toward him. The weightlessness he felt when he bounded over to the window in time to see the asteroid. He wondered if this was what Sera used to feel when she had her Remnants.

"Sometimes, when I gaze at the sky," Sera went on, "I feel like I'm looking into eternity. Do you ever feel like that, Dak?"

He shrugged because he didn't know how to answer. Sera was back to acting weird.

"Try it," she said. "Look up and tell me what you see."

Just as Dak raised his head to look at the sky, Sera lunged at him with her syringe.

He was ready for it, though, and just as the needle came at his neck, he raised his arm to block it. The needle stuck him in the forearm instead, and before Sera was able to drive in all the sleeping agent, the needle broke off in Dak's skin, and he pulled it out and tossed it into the snow. A third of the liquid had entered his arm, at most, but his brain still began to fog over. And his movements felt lethargic.

Sera pounced on him easily, pinning his arms under her knees. "You're going to be okay," she whispered in his ear. "We'll talk it over when you wake up in the USSR."

"U . . . ?" He tried to ask what she was talking about, but he couldn't. His tongue felt like a dead fish in his mouth. His eyelids drooped.

The fog grew even thicker in Dak's brain, and he closed his eyes. The dose hadn't been strong enough to knock him out completely. He pretended, though, to buy himself time to think. Otherwise he was afraid Sera would stick him with her second needle. And then he'd be asleep for days.

There was a commotion near the rocket. And Dak could feel Sera shifting her body to look. He cracked open his eyes, just a fraction. Everything was blurry. And jittery. But he saw a flash of gold from inside her knapsack, just out of his reach.

"Thirty seconds to launch," the flying disk announced.

Sera turned back to Dak, and he shut his eyes just in time. She slapped him across the face, saying, "You asleep, Dak? Hey, nerd boy? Can you hear me?"

Dak didn't move or say a word.

He just lay there, barely breathing.

She slapped him a second time, and he still didn't move, even though his heart was breaking.

"Good," she said, getting off him. "At least I know how to shut you up now."

Dak heard her fumbling with her second syringe and then he heard her step out from behind the tree, shouting across the farm, "Tie them up! I'll handle the rocket myself!"

Dak cracked open his eyes. The world was spinning on him now. He saw tiny stars everywhere and he wondered if they were the microscopic cells that made up the world. He scooted his way to the right a few inches and snatched the Ring from Sera's knapsack and shoved it down his pants and closed his eyes again, wondering if that's what death was: You saw all the tiny molecules of life right before the life drained out of you, and then you were gone.

"Okay, Dacky Boy," Sera said, "you stay here while I make sure the AB Pacifists have everything they need. Then we're off to the Soviet Union."

Dak heard Sera tying up her knapsack and he heard the flying SQuare buzzing away from him and then he felt something warm cover the top half of his body. When he heard Sera crunching through the snow away from him, Dak opened his eyes and saw that she had placed her jacket over him, to keep him warm.

His mind was in such a fog now, it was hard to form a coherent thought. But he knew he was hidden behind a tree so he slowly sat up, sucking in difficult breaths, and felt around him for the Ring. It took him several minutes to remember it was in his pants, beneath his robe. He pulled it out and set it on the snow. He was so exhausted now he had to slap his own face to keep from passing out. He pinched his arm and pried open his eyes with his fingers.

Dak looked at the Ring, and then he looked at the jacket Sera had covered him with.

He was so confused.

Would someone who planned to do him harm really try to keep him warm?

He tried to focus on the Ring. It was spinning in his hand, though he knew it wasn't really spinning.

Where would he even go?

He felt like he was lost, without a friend or ally in all of history that he could turn to.

But that wasn't entirely true.

There was still Riq.

He struggled to program the device, then aimed a shaky forefinger at the ACTIVATE button, but he was seeing three of everything now.

He heard the sound of bodies falling in the distance.

Dak had no idea which ACTIVATE was the right one, so he pushed them all, and everything around him began to spin more dramatically and the world went black, like his mind, and he knew it wasn't from the warp this time. It was the drug Sera had injected into his throbbing arm.

PART THREE

Tamales from Scratch

SERA DIDN'T sleep at all the night she spotted the drone out the window. It wasn't that she was scared of some Frisbee-size hunk of flying aluminum. She just wanted to know who was behind it. And the more she tossed and turned, thinking about it during the night, the more she kept circling back to one disturbing possibility.

Her parents.

She knew they had the tech skills to do it. But did they have the motivation? Wherever they had disappeared to, had they decided to keep an eye on her while they were away? If so, she doubted they were acting out of parental concern. What if they had sent the drone to the barn to find out what she was working on in case it was something they needed to report back to the SQ about?

The idea alone was soul crushing, and Sera didn't want to believe it. But part of her did. At first light, she decided to spend the day combing through every inch of the house, her new dog right by her side, in case her parents had left anything lying around that might give her some answers.

This was *not* what Sera had in mind all those years she'd dreamed of having her parents in her life. *Be careful what you wish for,* she remembered her uncle always telling her. But he was talking about the dangers of scientific advancement. A saying like that should *never* apply to someone's own mom and dad.

Sera had already searched all the bedrooms and both bathrooms and the shed out back and the living room and the kitchen, and she still hadn't found anything too suspicious. The only thing that was remotely questionable was the wax paper she found wadded up in the garage trash can. It was the paper her dad had used during the strange spitting game he'd insisted they all play during their dinner with Dak. There were two holes in the paper, like her dad had cut out the parts where their saliva had landed.

"Ew," she said, plopping down on the couch. "What would he want with somebody's *spit?*"

The dog barked in agreement.

Sera was just about to start rifling through the downstairs bookshelf when the doorbell rang. She stood up, crumpling the wax paper, and hid it behind the couch.

The bell rang a second time and as Sera started across the living room, the dog still following closely behind her, a familiar voice called out from the other side of the door.

She undid the chain lock and pulled open the door. "Dak?"

"Sera!" he said, a little too excitedly. He was wearing a backpack she'd never seen, and the big grin on his face put her on guard. He pushed past her into the living room, saying, "I'm glad I found you, Sera. We have so much to talk about."

"We do?" Sera said.

"Of course we do." Dak knelt down to pet the dog. "Hey, buddy. You missed me, didn't you?"

The dog growled.

Sera watched this odd exchange, feeling about as confused as she'd ever been. "I thought you *hated* my dog," she said.

"Not at *all*," Dak said, standing up.

"But yesterday—"

"She's a survivor, Sera. Like me and you." When Sera didn't say anything right away, Dak added, "We will always accomplish what we set out to accomplish. You know that, right?"

"I know you're acting like a freak," Sera told him. "What's with the backpack?"

"I'm glad you asked," he said, walking over to the couch and sitting down. He pulled the backpack off his shoulder and unzipped it. "I brought you a little gift. Three gifts, actually."

Now Sera had moved beyond confused. She was *concerned*.

Dak had never, ever brought her a gift out of the blue like this. Which meant it had to be another ploy to get what he wanted. What else could explain Dak being so ... nice?

Sera took the box he was holding out to her and lifted off the top. She was shocked to find three brand-new petri dishes wrapped in delicate tissue paper. She looked up at Dak. "How'd you know I needed these?"

Dak tilted his head. "Sera, it's pretty obvious things haven't been going so well in the barn. The trash is about ten feet away from my hammock, remember?"

Sera pictured all her batches of failed tachyon fluid. Maybe Dak was a little more perceptive than she gave him credit for.

Dak then pulled a book out of his bag. "I also brought this for you, but it's for later."

Sera saw the title: *The Principia* by Isaac Newton. A book that had changed her life in fourth grade. When she reached for it, Dak quickly shoved it back in his bag.

"Like I said," he told her, "that's for later. But *this* isn't." He then produced a brown paper bag. "I cooked a little something for you, too. It's a sort of peace offering. I really shouldn't have brought up Riq yesterday, Sera. I'm sorry."

"Okay, this is getting to be a bit much," Sera said, unfolding the top of the lunch bag. "Petri dishes. One of my all-time favorite books. And now"—she looked inside—"shut up, are these tamales?"

"Traditional *Mayan* tamales," Dak corrected her. "I made them from scratch."

Sera sniffed inside the bag of tamales. They actually smelled legit. "Okay, what's the catch?" she asked.

"Just take a bite," he told her.

Sera did just that, nodding as she chewed. "Wow, Dak," she said with her mouth still half full. "This is really, really good. I'm shocked." She swallowed and said, "Seriously, though, what's the catch?"

Dak took a deep breath. "Well, actually—"

"I knew it," Sera interrupted.

The dog growled at Dak and showed her teeth.

"Trust me," Dak said. "You'll want to hear this. I have some important information about your parents."

"My *parents*?" Sera's stomach sank.

Dak nodded. "They're gone, aren't they? They've been gone for a while now."

Sera set down the bag of tamales. "How'd you know that?"

"You think I just sit around all day, but I work, too, Sera. In fact, yesterday I spoke to Arin. You remember her, right?"

"Of course I do," Sera told him. "But I doubt she remembers us."

"She *absolutely* remembers us," Dak said. "Arin works for a small, secret division of the Hystorians. And you're not gonna believe what she told me."

"What?" Sera said. "Tell me!"

Dak looked around the room, like he was making sure they were the only ones around.

Sera's dog snapped her teeth a few times and snarled. "Easy, girl," Sera said, reaching down to rub her furry head.

"According to Arin," Dak continued, "we actually *haven't* fixed all the Breaks. We have to go back to seventeenth-century Italy, to the trial of Galileo."

Sera gasped. Galileo was one of her heroes. His guiding principle was to follow knowledge wherever it led. No matter what. And that's the exact kind of scientist Sera had always wanted to be.

Dak nodded. "And then she gave me *this*."

Sera watched Dak pull out the Infinity Ring. Only it wasn't silver, like the one she'd hidden. It was gold. "All right," she said, feeling anxious all of a sudden. "And what does any of this have to do with my parents?"

Dak pointed at the tamale. "Eat up and follow me. I'll show you."

Sera didn't know what was happening or what to think. She just knew she had to find out the truth. So she popped the rest of her tamale in her mouth and followed Dak out the door. The dog followed, too, hackles up.

When they arrived at the tree house Dak and Sera used to hang out in, back when life was simple, Dak nodded at the ground and said, "Go ahead, dig it up."

She was shocked he knew where she'd hidden the Infinity Ring. She lifted a few weeds and dug with her hands until she came to the tin box she'd buried weeks before. She lifted it out and opened it, and her stomach dropped. It was filled with worthless rocks.

The Infinity Ring was gone.

Sera looked up at Dak. "My parents did this?"

He nodded. "Have you seen a drone hovering around the barn lately?"

"I have!" Sera said. "Just yesterday! Please don't tell me . . ."

"Your parents, Sera." Dak shook his head sadly. "They've been spying on us. I'm sorry to be the one who breaks this to you, Sera, but they still support the SQ agenda. They've gone back to the trial of Galileo to rewrite history . . . and bring the SQ back in a big way."

Sera's breath caught. She knew her parents were up to something. But this was far worse than she'd imagined.

"I understand how tough this is to hear," Dak said. "But they have a huge head start on us. We have to warp back to the trial right away." He unfolded a piece of paper and handed it to Sera. "Here are the coordinates Arin gave me. I'll let you do the honors."

Sera felt devastated as she took the gold Infinity Ring and the piece of paper. She loved her parents, but she couldn't let them get away with undoing all the work she and Dak and Riq had done.

She programmed the golden Ring with a heavy heart and watched the computerized screen flash their destination: ROME, JUNE 22, 1633. Right before the Age of

Enlightenment. But she couldn't even be excited about it.

"Grab on," she told Dak.

He gripped the far side of the Ring and nodded to her.

Sera hit the ACTIVATE button, but just as everything was starting to spin, she saw her nameless dog reach a paw up for the Ring, too, barking, and the three of them were sucked into the dark abyss together.

Scientific Superstar
in the Flesh

IT WASN'T the dog's slobbery tongue lapping across Sera's face that woke her out of a dead sleep. It was the dog's awful breath. Sera's nose instinctively wrinkled and she popped open her eyes and nudged her dog's cold snout out of the way. She sat up, wiping her face on her shirtsleeve, saying, "No face licking, Ginger. Or Dixie. Or whatever your name is."

When the dog lowered her head in shame, Sera hugged her tightly and added, "I'm glad you came with me, though. We're a team now."

The dog licked her face again, and this time Sera let it slide.

Sera got up from her simple cot to investigate her surroundings. She was in a small, dark room with heavy beige curtains, white walls, and dark wooden floors. Other than the large, gaudy cross above the door, the room was incredibly plain.

Was this really seventeenth-century Rome? What happened to all the . . . stuff?

And why was she so exhausted?

Sera heard people shouting in Italian outside so she went to the window and brushed aside the curtains to look. There were two groups of men in what looked to be some kind of town square. They were arguing and pointing at each other. One group was dressed in the black robes that she knew Roman Catholics called cassocks. They had matching black hats. The other group was dressed in more modern-looking trousers and long shirts. They looked like students.

And then Sera spotted the smallest of the trouser-wearing crew. He was standing right in the middle of the action, shouting louder than anyone else and in perfect Italian.

Dak.

Sera threw on the clothes Dak had clearly left for her and rushed out the door, the dog following closely behind. She pushed her way into the crush of people and tugged at Dak's arm. "What are you doing?" she scolded him. "You're going to get trampled out here."

"Sera?" Dak was looking at her like he'd just seen a ghost. "Why aren't you still . . . sleeping?"

The argument around them escalated, and Sera realized why this felt so different from any of their previous warps. Because she wasn't wearing a translation device, she couldn't understand a word anyone was saying.

Dak let her pull him aside. Once they were a safe distance away from the two clashing groups, Sera asked, "How long was I asleep? And why didn't you wake me up?"

"Only a few hours," Dak said. "You seemed sick or something, so I thought it was best to let you rest."

The dog growled at Dak and showed her teeth.

Sera agreed with the dog: Dak was being sketchy. She narrowed her eyes at him. When was the last time he'd left her alone just because she was a little under the weather? *Never*, that's when. Dak didn't pay attention to stuff like that. He had to be up to something.

"You should have woken me up," Sera snapped. "What are we doing here? What have I missed?"

Dak shouted a few more lines of Italian at the men in black cassocks before turning back to Sera. "Are you familiar with the heliocentric theory?" Dak asked her.

"Duh," Sera answered. "The heliocentric theory states that the Earth revolves around the sun — not the other way around. I wrote about it on my blog two years ago. Remember? You left a comment suggesting that the Earth revolves around cheese."

"Oh," Dak said. "I mean, I forgot. Anyway, Galileo has been promoting the heliocentric theory all over the place lately, and now he's been called in for an inquisition."

"Right," Sera said, recalling the significance of the date she'd entered into the Infinity Ring. "This is the day they find him guilty of heresy, right?"

Dak nodded excitedly. "It's history in the making, Sera. In order to stay out of jail, Galileo is going to be forced to publicly declare that he was mistaken—"

"What a joke!" Sera shouted. "All of Galileo's research is supported by the most powerful telescope available at the time. He *proved* the Earth revolves around the sun. It's one of the most absurd setbacks in the history of scientific progress!"

Dak looked genuinely frightened by her anger.

"Sorry." She took a deep breath and let it out slowly. "You know how I get when it comes to this stuff."

Dak took a step closer and told Sera in a much quieter voice, "You're right to be upset. In history as we know it, the cardinals rule against Galileo. We're here because we can't let that happen." He opened up his backpack and pulled out the copy of Isaac Newton's *The Principia* and handed it to her. "How familiar are you with this book?"

"Are you kidding?" Sera said. "I basically have it memorized."

"Good," Dak said, "because you're going to use it to prove Galileo's position is valid."

"What?" Sera said. "How?"

"I've already set everything in motion for you," Dak told her. "You just have to trust me on this one."

But that was the problem. Sera didn't know if she *could* trust Dak anymore. He'd been acting strange from the moment he'd shown up at her parents' house. And now there was this look in his eyes she didn't recognize. And there had to be a reason her dog was still snarling at her best friend and emitting a low growl. Animals sensed when people were hiding something.

Sera would have started drilling Dak with additional questions if at that exact moment, everyone in the town square hadn't gone utterly silent.

Sera looked up and saw a group of armed soldiers escorting a man in shackles toward the courthouse.

A buzz of voices rippled through the square as the shackled man was led right past Sera and Dak. He looked up and met eyes with Sera, and Sera's heart began pounding so fast, she wondered if this was what it felt like to have a heart attack.

This was her idol, Galileo.

In the flesh. In chains.

She actually had to remind herself to breathe.

When the man was led through the doors of the courthouse, Dak tapped the book in Sera's hands. "The entire course of history is counting on you," he said.

"No pressure," Sera mumbled to herself, still staring at the doors of the courthouse. She swallowed hard, remembering that ten cardinals would rule Galileo guilty. How was she going to convince them that the Earth revolved around the sun when they were so set in their ways, they had refused to even look through Galileo's telescope?

The Trial

SEVERAL HOURS later, Sera found herself standing outside the courtroom, where she and Dak argued with a dozen armed guards who refused to even let them inside. Actually, it was just Dak doing the arguing. Sera couldn't understand a word anyone was saying, and the daggers she was staring at the men didn't seem to be having much of an effect.

Sera had spent the day in her small room with her dog, reviewing Isaac Newton's masterpiece, *The Principia*. Only it wasn't considered a masterpiece in seventeenth-century Rome because it had yet to be written. Isaac Newton hadn't even been born yet. So every sentence in the book would be unfamiliar to the cardinals. Sera couldn't decide if that was a good thing or a bad thing.

Of course, it was a moot point if Sera couldn't even get into the courtroom. She watched as Dak went from arguing in a calm, rational way to shouting, but the guards continued shaking their heads and shooing Dak and Sera away.

"What now?" Sera asked Dak when he turned his back on the men, shaking his head, too. The trial was nearly over.

"I don't understand why they're not here yet," Dak said, looking over Sera's shoulder.

"Who?" Sera wanted to know. "And what did you just say to the guards?"

Dak turned to Sera, his face red with anger. "They don't know who they're dealing with, Sera. I'm tight with this pacifist group, the AB. As soon as they find out I was mistreated, they're going to—"

"Who's the AB?" Sera interrupted. "How come I've never heard of them?"

Dak's face grew uncertain, like he'd just let something slip that he'd meant to keep to himself. "It's just this group that helps, you know . . . I met them while you were asleep. They're the ones who hooked us up with the clothes we're wearing."

"But who *are* they?" Sera asked. "And why are they helping you?"

Her dog barked at Dak and continued her low growling.

"Maybe I'm just a likable guy," Dak said, looking down at the snarling dog. "Right, girl?"

The dog snapped her teeth at Dak. This time, Sera actually had to hold her dog back. Before she could ask

Dak any more questions, a group of four robust men dressed in black cassocks approached the guards. One of them waved to Dak and said something in Italian.

"Thank heaven," Dak responded.

"What?" Sera asked. "What is it?"

Dak turned to her. "They're going to take care of us."

"Is it the AB group you were talking about?"

Dak nodded.

As the men spoke to the guards in deep, authoritative voices, Sera studied the gold trim of their cassocks. She'd never seen a priest wear gold before. It almost seemed too flashy for church. It reminded her of the gold Infinity Ring they had used to warp here, and she wondered if Arin back home had anything to do with the AB. Maybe the smaller Hystorian group had taken on a different name.

Sera was shocked when the guards suddenly stepped aside and allowed the men in gold-trimmed cassocks to open the doors to the courtroom. The AB men bowed to Dak, which confused Sera even more, and waved them inside.

And then something happened that she did not expect at all. Out of nowhere, she felt faint and almost passed out. She had to go down on one knee so she wouldn't fall forward and smash her face on the ground. There was a weird ringing in her ears, too, and for a few seconds her mind went blank. But then she was fine again, like nothing happened.

height, all earthly objects fell towar

en tested his theory. And then h

r, suggesting that *every* object draw

d it, but the larger and heavier objec

he more powerful drawing powe

e will always fall toward the Eartl

rising up toward the apple.

Sera explained, the Earth is a millior

n apple, therefore its drawing powe

ronger.

and looked around the room.

re to be found.

nodding in support. And the cardi

tening.

n then applied this idea in a more

told them. "If the sun is a millior

eavier than the Earth, which Mr

d in his extensive telescopic research

have a draw that is a million times

id anything, she answered her owr

e it is. And that's what causes the

und the sun instead of the other way

ng to do with politics or religion anc

th science."

ices started spreading through the

"Come on," Dak said anxiously. "They're just about to issue their verdict. You do your thing, and I'll keep an eye out for unwanted guests." He stopped her near the back row of chairs and transferred the translation device, which was gold like the Ring, from his ear into Sera's. She felt the translator in her tooth, which Riq had inserted months ago, spark to life once the earpiece was in place. Dak winked at her — which was weird — and stepped back into the shadows just as one of the cardinals slammed his gavel against the table.

"We have our verdict," the man said in Italian.

Sera could understand him perfectly now. It was a little gross to think of Dak's earwax mixing with her own, but it was the only way she'd be able to present her argument.

"By majority vote," the cardinal went on, "we find the defendant, Galileo Galilei—"

"Wait!" Sera said, leaping out from behind the last row of chairs.

Everyone spun around to look at her. The courtroom was packed. She stepped forward, trying to appear confident, and stated, "Galileo is right about the heliocentric theory, and I can prove it!"

Two of the guards came rushing into the courthouse and took Sera by her arms, but one of the cardinals stood up and shouted, "Let the girl speak!"

Sera saw that while the rest of the cardinals were dressed in traditional cassocks, the robe of the man

"Furthermore," Sera said, "Isaac Newton believes the heliocentric theory is supported by his laws of gravitation, which I've hand-copied for all of you today. So you can see for yourselves." She began handing each cardinal a piece of paper with Newton's three laws of motion. "However, this doesn't mean the sun stays in a fixed position either. So you're both right in a way. All planetary masses are in constant motion."

The buzz inside the courtroom swelled even more, and one of the cardinals had to slam his gavel on the table to get everyone to quiet down.

When Sera was done passing out the pieces of paper to all the cardinals, she saw Galileo wave her over. Her heart sped up as she approached him. "Yes, sir?" she said tentatively.

"That was really something," he said. "Do you mind if I take a look at one of those?"

"Of course," Sera said, handing over her last copy of Newton's gravitational laws. She watched Galileo study the words and equations. She could almost imagine his great mind doing somersaults inside his skull.

After a couple of minutes, he looked up and said, "This is groundbreaking, young lady. I'd like to meet this Sir Isaac Newton fellow immediately. Can you arrange it?"

Sera's eyes grew wide with surprise. "Oh, well . . . he's really hard to reach at the moment, but —"

Luckily, she was interrupted by one of the cardinals, who was pounding his gavel again. "All rise," he announced. "In light of this new testimony, we've decided to suspend our decision until an academic committee can properly study this new theory called . . ."

"Gravity," Sera said.

"Yes, gravity," the man said. "Galileo is free to go."

The Kick that Ended a Friendship

SOME PEOPLE in the courtroom booed. Others cheered. And then a group of people near the back began chanting Galileo's name in this strange, drawn-out way that Sera thought would be more appropriate at a professional sporting event than in a courtroom.

"Ga-li-le-o!"

"Ga-li-le-o!"

"Ga-li-le-o!"

Sera was surprised to see the man pointing up into the crowd and pumping his fist. He jumped up on one of the tables and shouted, "It moves! I'll repeat it until my dying day! The Earth moves, do you hear me? It moves!"

This proved to Sera she had altered history forever. Instead of having to rescind his belief in the heliocentric theory, Galileo was shouting it from the rooftops. Or at least the tabletops. He even went over to a group of young women and kissed all their hands in an incredibly flirtatious way.

Interesting, Sera thought. *Galileo is a player.*

She shook the thought from her head and decided to go in search of Dak. It was probably a good idea to get out of the courtroom before anyone figured out that Isaac Newton didn't even exist yet. She looked all around the crowded courtroom but didn't see Dak anywhere.

Her dog was gone, too.

She broke into a cold sweat and began walking up and down each row, searching for them. She squeezed through a large group of celebrating students, deciding to try behind the stage. The first thing she saw was the group of men in gold-trimmed cassocks, standing around in a circle.

And then she noticed what was inside that circle.

Her dog.

"Again!" someone called out, and she knew right away it was Dak's voice. One of the men took a couple of steps forward and kicked her dog right in the ribs.

She howled in pain.

"What are you doing?!" Sera shouted.

Dak spun around. He was wearing his green back-pack, like he was already prepared to leave. "Sera," he said, "I thought you were with Galileo—"

"I'm right here!" she shouted back. "Obviously." She was so angry, she marched right up to Dak and pushed him onto the ground. The top of his backpack flew open and all of its contents went sliding across the floor, including the golden Infinity Ring and the bag full of Mayan tamales.

Dak looked up at Sera and then turned to the men and shouted, "Seize her!"

Sera's mouth fell open.

Had Dak really just ordered them to capture her — in flawless Italian?

As the men in gold-trimmed robes approached her, Sera had an epiphany of her own, not unlike the epiphany Isaac Newton had after watching an apple fall from an apple tree.

The gold Infinity Ring.

The gold-trimmed cassocks.

The gold translation device.

The cardinal who was so anxious to hear her testimony.

And most important, the tamales Dak had fed her. The ones that had made her fall asleep on the job. Was it possible that he'd laced them with some kind of sleeping pill?

This wasn't the Dak she'd known all her life. Someone had brainwashed him, flipped him onto the side of evil. She didn't understand who could have done this or how, but she trusted her instincts.

She was on her own now.

One of the AB Pacifists reached out to grab Sera's arm, and she ducked. But he managed to catch the side of her head, ripping out Dak's gross, earwaxy translation device. *Good riddance,* Sera thought as she slipped beyond the reach of the rest of the men and hurried toward the back exit, pausing only to scoop up the gold Infinity Ring.

She booked it out of the courthouse.

Sera raced back around the building and across the town square, her poor dog limping alongside her and whimpering. The two of them kept running until they were at the end of a quiet, vacant road, where Sera knelt down behind an empty carriage, out of breath, and tried to think. She could hear a very vocal crowd coming her way, but she couldn't see them . . . yet.

She stared at the golden Infinity Ring. If it were just Dak, she would try and talk to him. Maybe she could bring him back to his true self. But that was impossible while he was surrounded by thugs. No, she'd have to warp somewhere without him, and she'd have to do it now.

But where would she go?

Home wasn't an option. Her parents were gone, and even if they were sitting on the couch right now, waiting for her return, she didn't trust them. For all she knew, they were the ones who'd turned Dak against her.

Finally, it dawned on Sera. The one person she knew she could trust was Riq.

But where would she go to find him?

"There she is!" someone shouted in the distance.

Sera looked up and found Dak racing toward her, followed by his posse of gold-wearing priests. "Stay right where you are!" he shouted as he and his men closed in on her.

Suddenly, it hit Sera like a ton of bricks. She'd go back to southern Anatolia in 333 BC, just after the Battle of Issus. Riq would still be there on orders from Alexander the Great. Dak had said as much himself.

But was that before or after he'd turned against her?

There was no time to run through all the possibilities in her head. She had to act *now*.

Sera programmed the Ring as quickly as possible and hugged her wounded dog to her side. Then she slammed her hand down on the ACTIVATE button.

The last thing she heard was Dak yelling, "No! You'll ruin the moon!" And she saw him fall to his knees, shouting toward the heavens.

Then everything began spinning around her, and she was lost inside the warp.

15

When It Rains, It Pours

SERA CRASH-LANDED out of her warp right onto the back of a grizzled Macedonian warrior wielding a shield and spear. He shouted something she couldn't understand while at the same time battling the two men in front of him. Sera wrapped her arms around his sweaty neck and hung on for dear life. The spear of one of the opposing men whizzed by Sera's right eye. An arrow stuck in the ground next to her warrior's feet.

The action was way too close for comfort, and she let out a scream in the man's ear.

Her dog howled in the distance.

"Daisy!" she shouted. "Ginger! I'm over here!"

War raged all around Sera. Tens of thousands of men engaged in battle on a cold, rainy day. Hundreds were already motionless on the ground, or in the small Pinarus River that ran right through the fight, clouds of red puffing out in the tide.

Sera had to get out of the fray or she'd be killed.

But how? And why had she warped right into the red-hot center of the Battle of Issus? She remembered from reading about Riq—known as Hephaestion now—that Alexander the Great was leading his army against Darius and his Persian army, which was far superior in numbers. But reading about a war was way different from finding herself in the heat of the battle, surrounded by death and rage and violence. Arrows screamed through the air. Spears clinked against shields. Horses galloped by, with armored warriors swinging lances. But what disturbed Sera most was the sound of grown men screaming.

She stopped looking around. It was too overwhelming. She had to concentrate on these three men, on getting safely to the ground and picking up the golden Ring, which lay on a patch of wet grass a few feet away. If she didn't grab it soon, it would be trampled and she'd be stuck here forever.

Just as she was preparing for her dismount, though, her warrior overtook one of his opponents, sinking his sword into the man's shoulder and quickly ripping it back out. The man collapsed to the ground, holding his wound and shouting curses in some foreign tongue. The man fighting at his side scurried off to a different part of the battle.

Before Sera knew what was happening, she'd been flipped over her warrior's back and slammed onto the ground, and the tip of a bloody sword was aimed at her heart.

The Macedonian shouted down at her, but she couldn't understand a word he was saying. "I'm sorry I landed on you!" she shouted back. "I'll go now!"

But she was wasting her breath.

They'd never be able to communicate.

The man lowered the sword so that the tip was pressing against the white Roman blouse she was wearing—which she knew made her stick out like a sore thumb.

"Hephaestion!" she shouted in desperation. "He's my friend!"

The man's face changed.

The pressure of the sword eased up a little, and Sera pulled in quick, anxious breaths.

"Hephaestion?" the warrior said.

"Yes!" Sera shouted. "Take me to him! He'll explain everything, I promise."

She knew the man couldn't understand, but he seemed to get the gist of it because his eyes softened. They were friends with the same man. Hephaestion. Riq. A great man, whatever you chose to call him. Sera and Dak had read about all the amazing things he had done—and would do.

The Macedonian warrior took the sword away completely and held a hand out for Sera. Her breath caught as she reached up for it. Because she was safe for now. And she'd be taken to Riq. And the two of them could figure out what to do about Dak . . . *and* her parents.

Just as their hands met, however, a Persian soldier

hurrying past them stabbed Sera's warrior right in the back.

His hand went limp.

His eyes grew wide with fear as he continued staring at Sera. Then they drifted off to the side, and he collapsed right onto her, dead.

Sera climbed out from under him and checked his pulse and then screamed up at the heavens. Because what had just happened was all her fault.

Her dog howled again in the distance.

Sera pulled herself together, picked up the warrior's sword and the muddy Infinity Ring, and moved through the battle, hardly thinking now. She just knew she had to find her dog and get off the battlefield somehow. Then she'd figure out what to do next.

She jabbed her sword in the direction of a few of the warriors she passed, men from both sides, but she didn't try to hurt anyone. She just wanted to look the part. Mostly, though, people ignored her.

Sera found her dog pinned under a fallen horse. The dog whined pitifully, and Sera panicked for a moment, fearful that her companion was hurt. She was able to push the horse enough for her dog to wiggle out, though, and she was pretty sure that nothing was broken. The dog danced on her paws and yipped, happy to see Sera but clearly anxious, too, as the battle raged all around them.

Sera led her down the slick bank, toward the river

water, thinking they'd be able to walk along the stones sticking up out of the shallow water.

"How are we ever going to find Riq in this mess?" she asked her dog as they both struggled along the shore, slipping every few steps. It was impossible. She'd warped to the wrong date. But what was the *right* date? The history books all said the Battle of Issus ended sometime in November 333 BC. How was she to know what the actual day was if the history books couldn't be any more specific?

Warping without having a team of Hystorians behind her was an entirely different experience. Normally, she'd be able to track down an actual Hystorian or figure out a riddle on the SQuare or, at the very least, rely on Dak's knowledge.

Today, she was out here all alone.

About a hundred yards down the narrow, muddy trail, a wounded Persian warrior stepped out from the darkness ahead of her and shouted something she couldn't understand. He raised his sword in his left hand, challenging her, and Sera saw that his right arm hung limp and bloodied by his side.

"I don't want any trouble!" Sera shouted back. "I just want to pass!"

The wounded man began approaching her, waving his sword threateningly.

Sera backed up, pulling her dog back by the scruff of her neck. She would have made a run for it, but she was trapped between the water on one side of the narrow trail, and the steep bank on the other side, which was twice her height at this point.

Rain continued falling.

Sera shivered in the cold wind as she retreated, never taking her eyes off the man. A part of her wished she was still in Rome, with Dak. She could have pretended everything was perfectly normal, bided her time until she figured out why Dak had been acting so strangely. If she could have just talked to him one-on-one, she was sure she could have brought him back to his true self.

But then she remembered how Dak had ordered the men in gold-trimmed cassocks to kick her dog. That was the one thing she didn't think she could ever forgive.

On cue, her dog barked, and Sera saw that the wounded warrior had broken into an awkward jog toward her. The man was injured to the point that Sera was pretty sure she could take him. He was staggering as he ran, one arm dangling useless. And he'd clearly lost a ton of blood. But she didn't want to take anyone right now. Not when she already felt responsible for what happened to the Macedonian warrior she'd fallen on.

Instead of confronting the Persian man, she turned and hurried back the way she'd come, her dog splashing in the water as she ran alongside her.

They climbed the bank at its shortest point and Sera

saw that many of the Persian warriors were retreating, led by a man who had to be King Darius III. It was a strange sight, considering the Persians greatly out-numbered the Macedonians, but Alexander the Great had brilliantly used the lay of the land, broken up by the river, to his benefit.

The rain came harder as the fighting ceased, and Sera saw the true tragedy of war. There were fallen men everywhere. Many were motionless. Others lay wounded, shouting for help, the mud around them red with blood. Horses wandered aimlessly and a few men staggered past Sera, dragging their bloody swords behind them and staring vacantly ahead.

In the distance, Sera saw a group of men on horse-back gathering up Persian soldiers who had surrendered or been left behind, wounded. And then they turned toward her.

Sera started backing away as the horses closed in on her. It was her clothes. They thought she was the enemy. She turned to run when they were less than twenty yards away, but there was nowhere to go. A few Macedonian warriors were on that side of her, too, arrows ready in their bows.

Then one of the men on horseback shouted some-thing in a powerful voice, and everyone stopped.

Sera spun around to look at that man, and her heart started pounding inside her chest.

It was Riq. Or Hephaestion.

She was saved.

He barked another order at his men, and two of them, both on horseback, trotted toward her. The first one picked her up by the back of her shirt and threw her over the front of his horse. Another man captured her dog in a large net and began dragging her away.

"No!" Sera shouted. "That's my dog!"

But the men didn't even slow down.

Sera turned to Riq, horrified, and shouted, "What's happening? What did you tell them to do?"

Riq removed his helmet and looked Sera over for a few long seconds. He was a little bit older than when she'd last seen him, taller and broader with a new fierceness in his brown eyes. "I told them to throw you in jail," he said in a cold voice she hardly recognized. "Because that's where you belong."

"What?" Sera said, a wave of panic spreading through her entire body. "Riq, it's me. Sera."

Riq didn't even bother answering this time. He tapped his horse with his foot and started galloping away.

Sera was in shock as one of the men on foot came up to her and wrestled away the golden Infinity Ring.

"No!" she cried. "Tell Riq—I mean, Hephaestion—I need that!"

But she knew her words were meaningless. They didn't understand her, and even if they did, Riq was the one who'd ordered her to be thrown in jail. As the horse she was on began trotting toward the end of the field,

Sera wracked her brain to try and figure out what had just happened. The only thing she could think of was that Riq had been brainwashed somehow. Turned against her. Just like Dak.

And there was only one party who could be responsible.

Her parents.

PART FOUR

Who Will Do the Honors?

WHEN SERA heard the guards coming, she stood up and went to the uneven metal bars, and listened to the sound of their footsteps coming down the hall, like she always did. She'd been in the Macedonian jail for five days now, and they still hadn't told her what crime she'd committed — not that she would have understood the guards' explanation anyway. Without a translator device, it all just sounded like ancient gibberish.

What bothered her most, though, was the fact that Riq still hadn't come to visit her. She was beginning to think there was no one left she could trust.

Not Riq.

Not Dak.

Not her parents.

She'd never felt so alone in her life.

"Take me to Hephaestion!" she shouted when the footfalls grew closer. She heard the usual two sets of feet, but this time she also heard a strange dragging sound. One of her prison mates, an old man with long gray hair and a gray beard, shouted something back at Sera. He'd been shouting at her since she'd arrived, and since she couldn't understand him, she no longer even acknowledged him. There were five other prisoners in the cell with her. Two Persian war prisoners, two Macedonian street thieves, and the old man. She kept as far away from them as possible during the day and slept sitting against the wall with one eye open.

Sera backed away from the metal bars as the guards finally came into view. They weren't bringing dinner like she had expected, though. They were dragging another prisoner toward the cell.

His head was bowed, and he was wearing a strange Asian robe that didn't at all match the time period. And then Sera glanced down at this new prisoner's shoes.

A pair of checkered Vans.

Her breath caught.

She watched the guards unlock the heavy door and swing it open and dump the limp body onto the brick floor. They promptly locked the cell door behind them and disappeared down the long hall.

Sera stared down at the small body lying by her feet. His oversized robe had flown up over his head, so she couldn't see his face, but he had on a modern pair of jeans and a T-shirt. And those Vans. Not exactly what you'd expect in ancient Anatolia. But how could this be? She'd left Dak back in seventeenth-century Rome without a time-travel device.

She slowly kicked the robe off the boy's face and her entire body went cold.

It was Dak, all right.

The old man was on his knees now, shouting up at the roof of the cell and pointing at Sera and Dak.

She kicked the robe back over her ex–best friend's face and moved as far away from him as possible, sitting against the opposite wall to try and think. How had he gotten here? And why was he wearing an ancient Chinese robe? And what was wrong with him? And why wouldn't this old man give it a rest?

Sera sat there for over an hour, waiting for Dak to wake up.

The guards brought dinner, a watery stew with some unidentifiable meat Sera refused to eat.

After they removed the food, the daylight that had been flooding through the small cell window began fading away.

The rest of the prisoners soon fell asleep, even the old man, but not Sera. She stared at Dak's motionless body, vowing to keep *both* eyes open tonight. There was no way she was going to let her guard down now.

Sera woke with a start and found Dak standing over her. She scrambled to her feet and got into a fighting position, fists clenched, ready to defend herself. How could this have happened? She'd only closed her eyes for a couple of seconds. But the entire cell was lit up by sunlight again. It had to have been longer.

Stupid! she thought.

"So, how'd you manage it?" Dak asked, getting into a fighting position of his own.

"Manage *what*?" Sera said, spitting out the words. Her brain was still slow from sleep, but she knew she had to focus, and fast.

"Getting me thrown into jail."

"Are you kidding?" Sera shouted. "The question is how'd you find me?"

They began slowly circling each other in the cell, staring at each other, waving around their fists. Sera watched Dak's mouth move as he talked, but she also watched his hips in order to pick up on any sudden movements so she'd be able to react in time.

"How'd I *find* you?" Dak countered. "I've been trying to get *away* from you!"

Sera picked up a broken piece of brick for protection. If it came down to it, she'd fire it right between Dak's eyes. Even if she missed her bull's-eye, his head was so big, she was bound to do some kind of damage.

Dak picked up a jagged board.

As they continued circling in the cell, never taking their eyes off each other, Sera stepped over the legs of the other prisoners, most of whom had begun to hoot and holler, excited to have some form of entertainment. Only the weird old man seemed to be pleading for peace.

"I'll never understand it!" Sera shouted at Dak. "How anyone could do that to their own best friend!"

"Me?" Dak scoffed. "I tried to give you the benefit of the doubt as long as I could, Sera. And then you tried to stab me—"

"I see you've been busy since I last saw you," she said, pointing at Dak's Chinese robe. "What animals did you harm over there?"

Dak spit, wielding his board like a sword. "Are you seriously gonna pretend you didn't stab me with that needle?" He pointed at his forearm, shouting, "Look at my arm, Sera! I'm bleeding like a stuck pig!"

Sera saw the small trickle of dried blood on his forearm. He'd always been a baby about cuts and bruises, but was he really blaming *her*? "I'll *never* forgive you for kicking my dog," she told him. "Why don't you come on over here, Dak? I'll show you what it feels like to get kicked in the ribs."

"Your *dog*?" Dak scoffed. "Is that what we're now calling that flying can opener?"

"You're not even making any sense!" Sera shouted.

"You've gone insane!" Dak fired back.

Sera's cell mates were all on their feet now, urging her and Dak to fight. They wanted blood. Anything to break up the monotony of sitting in jail all day doing nothing. And maybe they were right. Maybe Sera should just punch Dak in the nose and settle it that way. She was so tired and hungry and frustrated, she could barely form a coherent thought. And her words were coming out all jumbled. And didn't everyone always say that actions speak louder than words?

"I can look the other way about a lot of things," Dak growled between clenched teeth. "But you did the unforgivable, Sera. You ruined my taste for smoked Gouda. I can't even *picture* it now without feeling sick to my stomach."

"You used me to win a trial!" Sera countered. "And what thanks do I get? You chase me down like a wild animal."

Dak turned to the other prisoners. "Has she tried to stab any of you in the neck yet?" he shouted. "Because that's her new pastime! She especially likes stabbing old people!" He pointed at the man with the beard, who appeared to have tears on his cheeks.

Sera was so angry, she actually screamed.

A couple of the other prisoners laughed at her, which made Sera even *angrier.* She fired the brick at Dak's feet but missed. And then Dak charged at her and slammed his piece of wood against the wall right above her head. The wood fell from his hands and they grabbed on to each other's arms and tumbled onto the floor, Sera pulling Dak's hair and Dak pinching the skin on the back of her arm and twisting.

Dak leapt off her, shouting, "I knew it! You've been trying to kill me from the second we warped out of the forest!"

"Me?" Sera shouted back, climbing to her feet and rubbing her arm. "You've been trying to poison me with your stupid tamales since you showed up at my house. Oh, wait, I forgot. Your *Mayan* tamales. That was a nice touch, Dak! Using my ancestry against me!"

Dak spit again and shouted, "You're a liar, Sera Froste!"

"No, *you're* a liar, Dak Smyth!"

One of the other prisoners shouted something over their argument, and Sera looked at him. She turned back to Dak, saying, "Aren't you gonna tell me what he said? Or was that your plan all along? To have one of your thugs rip the translation device right out of my ear and leave me helpless?"

"*You're* the one with the stupid translation device!" Dak shouted back. "You tell *me* what he said!"

"Why don't I do the honors?" Sera heard a deep, manly voice say. She looked toward the prison door and saw someone standing there, someone tall enough that she could only see his chest through the metal bars.

But it was his perfect English that gave him away.

"I believe the literal translation would be, 'Shut up, you idiots. The guards are here.' And he was right on all counts. The guards are indeed here with me, and sadly you're both idiots." The owner of the voice then lowered himself enough for Sera to make out his face.

"Riq!" Dak shouted. "My man! It's been way too long. Get me out of here ASAP so we can discuss our next course of action."

Sera watched a big smile come over Riq's face. "Let you out?" he said. "Now, why would I want to do that? I'm the one who had you both thrown in here in the first place." He turned to the two guards he was with and said something in Greek. From the tone, Sera guessed it wasn't a request for extra pillows.

And with that, Riq began walking away from their cell.

Sera looked over at Dak, who was frowning so hard, his forehead was folding in on itself. He was just as angry and confused as she was. But there was something familiar in his eyes, too. Something she hadn't seen in days.

Whatever it was made her unclench her fists.

Still, it wasn't like she was going to *talk* to him after everything that had happened in Rome. She went clear to the other side of the cell and slid down the wall into a sitting position and watched him.

The old man was on his knees again, staring at the ceiling and preaching.

This time, Sera vowed not to let her eyes rest for even a second.

Double Duty

THE NEXT morning, Riq paced back and forth in his chambers, stressed out and exhausted. There were several people outside who needed to meet with him, but if he didn't take a second for himself, he was going to lose it.

They had been victorious in the Battle of Issus, yes, but he was starting to think victory brought as many headaches as defeat. Before Alexander the Great had headed down the Phoenician coast, he'd left Riq — better known around these parts as Hephaestion — in charge of appointing someone to the throne of Sidon, and it was a task Riq didn't take lightly. On top of that, he was in charge of realigning the Persian border and figuring out what to do with the ninety-seven remaining Persian war prisoners. He knew he was going to release them, but he hadn't figured out how to do it safely. He also had his own wounded warriors to look after. And on top of all that, Dak and Sera had decided that now was a good time to crash-land back into his life.

He used to think stress levels were high in the twenty-first century, especially when he had a big soccer match, or a test at school, but that was before he became the right-hand man of Alexander the Great.

The job accounted for his stress. The exhaustion came from his secret — and it was a big one.

For the past six weeks, Riq had been pulling double duty. He was, by day, Hephaestion, Alexander's best friend and top adviser, and by night, he was a time-traveling Hystorian who was slowly but surely uncovering some incredibly odd developments he had started to believe were the work of Tilda and what was left of the SQ.

In other words, Riq hardly ever slept.

He couldn't have known it at the time, but he was forever changed on the day he and Dak and Sera had finally defeated Tilda. In his anger with her, he'd shattered the woman's Eternity Ring — and tachyon fluid had splattered all over his bare hands and arms. Initially he was worried the fluid might be toxic, but Riq wasn't poisoned. It turned out the fluid had other effects entirely.

He figured it out one day by accident. He was taking a late-night stroll outside the castle he now lived in, when he started thinking about the Mayan girl from Izamal who had meant so much to him. Kisa. He remembered the date they'd last seen each other and he repeated it to himself in every language he knew that night. He was only trying to keep his language skills sharp. But when he mumbled the date in binary code, everything started swirling around him, and he blacked out. When he came to, he was in Izamal, 628 AD. And there was Kisa, sitting outside her hut all alone, eating something out of a clay bowl.

His stomach flooded with butterflies.

But he knew he couldn't speak to her. That might throw something off in the time continuum, and the last thing he wanted was to undo all the hard work he, Dak, and Sera had put into fixing the Breaks. He was nowhere near smart enough to figure out how it all worked, but he *was* smart enough to know not to tempt fate. So he settled for watching her over the course of the next few hours. He felt a little bit like a creep, but it was worth it. Because she was just as graceful and beautiful as he remembered.

And happy. It was good to see that she was happy.

He warped back to Anatolia that night before the sun came up over his new home city. It was easy, once he understood it. In essence, his entire body was an Infinity Ring now. He just had to program himself by speaking in code.

The following night, after he was done with all his duties, he opted for a different kind of warp. He went back to Athens to check up on Tilda, who had been left there, soundly defeated. Only Tilda was nowhere to be found. Instead, he heard rumors of a ghostly red-haired woman with a magical golden relic. People said they'd seen her vanish into thin air. And that's how his current wild-goose chase through time had begun.

He suspected that Tilda had somehow gained access to another time-travel device and had come up with a new plan, one that he was afraid might be more ambitious and sinister than anything before. He'd been racing through time — during his off hours — ever since, trying to uncover exactly what she was up to. But if Tilda was out there, she was keeping a low profile. Probably getting others to do her dirty work — like these AB Pacifists who seemed to be popping up everywhere.

There was another knock, and Riq started across the room toward the door. It looked like his quiet time was coming to an end.

He paused in front of the door, remembering the most troubling thing he'd learned during his six weeks of recon warps. Both Dak and Sera were actually *assisting* the AB Pacifists. But just last night, Riq had discovered what was really happening.

They had been tricked.

The knocking became more desperate, and Riq finally pulled open the door. It was two of his guards with a man he instantly recognized as Abdalonymus, the simple, trustworthy farmer he intended to crown king of Sidon — his last order of business before taking Dak and Sera on a little trip.

"Hello, there," he said, bowing in front of the man.

"Please, have a seat inside and I'll be with you in a moment."

The man gave a bow in return and went inside.

Riq stepped outside with his guards. "The two kids," he said, "have they killed each other yet?"

"Not yet," the larger guard said. "They're still staying as far away from each other as possible."

Riq grinned, picturing the two of them eying each other distrustfully all day. Wait until he told them the truth about how Tilda had been fooling them.

"They didn't get dinner, as you ordered. Should we feed them breakfast?" the smaller guard asked.

Riq rubbed his shoulder, where a small scar had begun to itch. He didn't remember where the scar had come from. He must have been cut in some battle.

He thought of his old friends, hungry in a cell.

What happened wasn't technically Dak's or Sera's fault. But they could have been quicker to figure things out—especially Dak. "I'll bring them food myself," he told the guards. "Get a basket together." Riq grinned to himself. "But no cheese."

The guards nodded and went off to perform their daily duties. Riq stepped back inside his office, readying himself to crown a new king.

A Different Kind of Warp

IT WAS early morning when Dak heard the guards shuffling down the hall, toward his cell. He stood up, eying Sera and the other prisoners. They were all still asleep. Dak rubbed his eyes, wondering how long he himself had been asleep. He'd vowed to stay awake through the night, but his exhaustion had gotten the best of him.

The door opened and in walked Riq, wearing a leather satchel and holding a large basket full of food. Dak's stomach immediately started growling. The thought of food was almost enough to make him forget how angry he was at Riq.

And Sera.

And just about everyone else he could think of.

Riq dismissed the guards and then turned to Dak and gave him a nod.

Dak was stiff from sleep, but that didn't stop him from staggering over to Riq. "I want answers," he demanded, getting in the bigger kid's face, "and I want them right this second."

"I'm sure you do," Riq said, leaning away from Dak. "I'd bet you want a toothbrush, too."

"And something to eat," Dak added. "Anything but smoked Gouda."

"Or tamales," Sera chimed in.

Dak turned around and saw that Sera was on her feet now, too. They watched each other uncertainly.

Riq set the basket on the ground. "There's fruit and bread and stuff in there. But I have to say, you guys aren't exactly in the best position to be making demands."

Dak dove into the basket first, grabbing a hunk of bread and a big stem of grapes. Sera reached in after him, followed by a couple of the other prisoners who had woken up, too. "What do you mean we shouldn't make demands?" Dak said between bites of the stale bread. "I didn't do *anything*."

"Please," Sera said, rolling her eyes. "*I'm* the one who's innocent."

They shot each other dirty looks.

All but one of the other prisoners were at the basket now. They were reaching in and pulling out the rest of the bread and fruits and olives and figs.

The loud old man with the wild gray hair and beard was back to his preaching again. He was on his knees, pointing at the stone ceiling of the cell and crying.

"What's he going on about anyway?" Dak asked.

Riq shook his head. "Some nonsense about the moon exploding. He was passed out in a ravine when my men picked him up." He motioned between Dak and Sera. "So, I take it there's not a whole lot of trust between you two right now."

"Me, trust *him*?" Sera said, pointing at Dak. "Not a chance."

Dak scoffed. "The feeling's quite mutual, my dear."

Riq was still grinning in this irritating way as he watched Dak and Sera wolf down their food. "How should I put this?" he said.

"What are you beating around the bush about?" Dak said, firing a grape at the older boy's legs. "Just say what you have to say. We deserve to know why you had us thrown in here in the first place."

"Exactly," Sera said. "We deserve the truth."

Dak and Sera looked at each other. It felt odd to be on the same side again — about *anything*. Dak looked away so she wouldn't start thinking they were friends again.

"The truth can be a dangerous thing sometimes," Riq said. "I'm not sure you're prepared for what I have to say."

Dak and Sera both stopped eating and shot him nasty scowls. Sera gave a little growl that actually kind of impressed Dak, so he growled, too.

"Okay," Riq said. "Fine. But don't say I didn't warn you." He took a deep breath and let it out slowly. "Remember our little friends from the SQ? The group we supposedly eliminated?"

Dak furrowed his brow at Riq. "What do you think, dude?" he said sarcastically. "We only risked our lives to stop them."

"Well, another group has risen up from their ashes," Riq said. "They call themselves the AB Pacifists. And I'm almost certain they're led by Tilda herself."

Dak almost choked on his food. He looked at Sera, remembering the men she'd been associating with in ancient China, and then Massachusetts. "By any chance, do these guys wear a lot of gold?" he asked Riq.

"As a matter of fact, they do."

Sera pointed at Dak. "You—!"

"Me?" Dak said, cutting her off. "More like *you*!"

"Hang on," Riq said. "It gets worse. The AB punked you *both*. They've been spying on you and your families from the minute you made it back to the present. From what I've gathered, they may have approached you separately with clone versions of each other. In other words, Dak, you were approached by a fake Sera. And, Sera, you were approached by a fake Dak."

Dak's eyes grew wide. "Clones?!"

He'd known there was something off about the Sera he'd just been warping around with, but he figured her parents had gotten to her somehow. He'd never even considered that he might be with Sera's evil clone.

"How?" Sera said. "There are only a few experts in the world who understand how cloning works. And they're nowhere near that level of sophistication." She sounded more impressed than horrified.

Riq shrugged. "I'm not exactly sure about that part yet. Or what Tilda's plan is. I just know it's up to us to stop her."

"Us?" Dak asked uncertainly. He looked at Sera and then looked at Riq again. A few hours ago, he'd decided there was no more "us." It surprised him how badly he wanted to believe Riq's outrageous explanation.

Dak watched Riq glance at the other prisoners, who had made off with the basket he'd brought in. The only one who wasn't huddled around it, wolfing down food, was the old man. Dak was still starving, but he wasn't exactly in the mood to argue over a few olives right now. He had a feeling Riq was about to drop another bomb on him and Sera.

"Yes, the three of us fixed all the original Breaks," Riq started. "And in doing so, we saved the planet from the Cataclysm. But Tilda's up to something else now. She's gone missing just as a new group of thugs has begun twisting events throughout time. I don't know what she's setting up exactly, but I do know she's been using *you* to help her cause. And from what I've gathered, she's just a few moves away from enacting the final stages of her plan."

"How do you know all this?" Dak asked.

"Never mind," Riq said. "There'll be time to discuss that later."

"I don't understand why they'd need us for any of

this," Sera said. "Wouldn't Tilda want to keep as far away from us as possible?"

"I don't fully understand it," Riq said. "But for some reason, all the traditional time-traveling devices have stopped working for the clones. Don't ask me why. The Ring was always keyed to your DNA, but clones should have the same DNA as you. Exactly the same. Anyway, in order for the AB to make their final few stops, they needed to trick you two into helping them. Which . . . didn't prove to be the most difficult task."

Dak walked toward the cell door, which was closed again, and locked. This was all too much to handle. How did Riq know all this? And was there really a Dak clone out there somewhere? And what were they supposed to do to stop Tilda when they no longer had a SQuare or Hystorians to help them? He spun around to Riq and said, "I've heard some crazy things in my life, but this . . . I mean, the idea of time travel alone is nuts if you actually stop and think about it."

"Not really," Sera said. "It's all just science. It only seems impossible until someone figures it out."

Dak threw his hand up in the air. "The point is, I'm having a real hard time wrapping my head around the idea of me and Sera having a clone."

Riq started laughing quietly.

"What now?" Dak said.

"Oh, you have more than just one clone," Riq said.

Sera wiped her hands down her face and said, "Why

do I have the feeling I'm not gonna like what you're about to say?"

"Because you're not," Riq said. "There's an entire clone factory of you guys on a small private island off the coast of twentieth-century Greece."

Dak almost choked on his last grape. He coughed and spit it out and stared at Riq. "Wait, *what?*"

"I'll prove it," Riq said.

Sera smacked her own forehead and said, "Let's take a step back here for a second. We destroyed Tilda's Eternity Ring. How is she leading *anything?*"

"I honestly don't know," Riq said. "But let me ask you guys something. Did you happen to notice anything a little out of the ordinary in the present? Before you went on your separate warps?"

Dak's eyes grew wide. "Dude, I saw a pterosaur in the forest," he said. "Or at least I thought I did. But then I just figured it was my mind playing tricks on me."

Riq grinned. "No, that was probably real."

"I saw this strange disk hovering in the air near the barn," Sera said. "Like it was—wait a second, are you telling me that was Tilda's people spying on me?"

"The fake you had one of those, too," Dak blurted out. "She called it her pet, ABe."

Riq took the leather satchel off his shoulder. He pulled it open and passed Dak and Sera each a gold Infinity Ring as well as a new translation device. "Here are your Rings back. Put the earpieces in now. You're gonna need to hear and see this for yourselves. Then we'll come up with a plan."

Dak followed Riq and Sera out of the prison cell, feeling his pulse quicken. In China, and then Massachusetts, he had felt so worthless. He was just standing on the sidelines while Sera — or who he *thought* was Sera — did all the work. But now he felt like he was needed again. And even though he didn't exactly understand what they were trying to stop, he knew it was something big, something important, and it made him feel like he mattered again.

He stood aside as Riq locked the door behind them, the other prisoners protesting in their ancient language. After a few seconds, his translation device kicked into gear, and he could actually understand what they were saying. Most of them were demanding that Riq let them out. But the old man was saying something completely different. "You have to listen to what I'm saying!" he pleaded. "The heavens! She claims she's going to take over the heavens!"

As Dak followed Sera and Riq down the long hall, he tried to wrap his head around the old man's message and everything else he'd just heard. The heavens. Clones. The AB Pacifists. New Infinity Ring technology. And then he recalled something that seemed like it could be related. Sera's dad had made them play that strange spitting game in the middle of dinner. What if he'd taken their spit back to Tilda? And what if that spit somehow factored into the production of these clones?

Dak watched Sera as they continued walking. He was no longer mad at her. In fact, he now felt sorry for her. Because it was possible that her parents were at the front lines of Tilda's new regime.

All the poor girl wanted was her family back. And look where that got her.

It didn't seem fair.

The three of them popped out into a courtyard, and Riq looked all around, making sure they were alone.

"What exactly do you know about these AB Pacifists?" Sera asked. "Are my parents . . . ?"

Dak was surprised that Sera had been thinking about the exact same thing.

"I'll explain everything I know," Riq said, "once we get to Santorini."

Dak frowned. "Santorini?"

"The Greek island we're about to visit." Riq scanned their surroundings again.

Dak and Sera both pulled out their gold Infinity Rings, but Riq waved them off, saying, "I got this one, guys."

"Since when do *you* have a Ring?" Dak asked.

"Technically, I don't," Riq said. "Now, grab on to my arms and hold on tight."

"Wait," Sera said. "What about my dog?"

"Don't worry," Riq said. "I gave her the run of my entire sleeping quarters. One of my guards is looking after her. Now, grab on."

Dak felt a little strange reaching out for Riq's arm, but he did it anyway. His chest flooded with excitement. He looked to Sera and nodded. And it made him happier than he expected when she nodded in return.

He had his best friend back.

Riq closed his eyes and tilted his head up toward the sky, and all of a sudden his entire body started shaking and his eyes vibrated behind his eyelids, like he was having some kind of seizure. Before Dak could even react, though, everything began spinning around them and he felt a familiar weightlessness come over his entire body. As they slipped into the darkness of their strange warp, Dak tried to imagine what he might find on the other side, but his thoughts were soon lost as he was sucked up into the void.

Before the War

SERA HAD never warped so many times in such a short amount of time, and it was starting to wreak havoc on her body. She had a dull headache now that followed her everywhere. And the tips of all her fingers and toes tingled. And this time, when she came to, in the middle of what looked like some kind of high school campus, there was a loud ringing in her ears.

She stood up and looked at Dak and Riq, who were both staring back at her, holding fingers in their ears.

So it wasn't just her.

The ringing sound stopped just as suddenly as it had begun.

"I take it that was some sort of school bell," Dak said.

Riq rubbed his temples, saying, "Of course it was a school bell. I warped us back to the AB Academy in 1955, on the island of—"

Before he could finish, the doors of the large building behind them swung open and a stream of students began rushing out, funneling around Sera, Dak, and Riq.

Sera's eyes grew wide as she focused in on their faces. "What the heck?" she managed to mumble under her breath.

Half of them looked exactly like her.

The other half, like Dak.

And all of them were wearing shiny gold bracelets.

As Sera stared at the endless stream of faces, her stomach felt like it was floating up into her throat, like it did when she went on roller coasters.

"Told you," Riq said.

The students were all hurrying past them, toward what looked to be some sort of cafeteria across the perfectly manicured lawn. They barely paid any attention to Sera, Dak, and Riq because they fit right in. At least Sera and Dak did. And Riq was with them. It was the first warp Sera had ever been on in which she wasn't the least bit worried about blending in.

She *was* these people.

She turned to Dak, whose mouth was hanging open like an old sock. It was the first time in ages she'd seen him speechless.

"They're all over the island," Riq said, waving his hand around. "There are literally hundreds of them. Thousands, maybe."

It was weird enough for Sera to be looking at clones of herself at her current age, but there were Seras of different ages, too. Kindergarten versions and third-grade versions and even high school versions. What freaked her out most of all were the adult versions who walked by, more leisurely. One of them, who looked like she was about fifty, even smiled at Sera and gave a little wink. It was like looking in a twisted fun-house mirror.

"Uh, you were right, Riq," Sera said. "I'm not sure I was ready for this."

Dak spun all the way around, looking at all of the students. "Well, at least now I know I age well," he said.

"Are you kidding me, Dak?" Sera barked. "We're standing here in a never-ending stream of our own clones and *that's* what you're focused on?"

"What?" Dak whined. "Look at this twenty-something me right here." He pointed toward an older Dak clone walking past them, arm in arm with an older version of Sera, eating string cheese. "Let's be honest. I turn out to be a handsome, handsome man. Check out that physique, Sera. I'm ripped."

All Sera could do was shake her head. "Please understand, Dak. The only reason the older me is walking so close to the older you is because there's not a whole lot else to choose from."

"Whatever you say," Dak told her. "Come here, let's hook our arms together and see if it's a good fit."

"Gross," Sera said. "I'd rather make out with my dog."

"Let's focus," Riq said. "Do you guys have any idea what all these clones are doing here?"

"Making the population a little smarter?" Dak said. "And easier on the eyes?"

Riq shot Dak a dirty look. "The AB Pacifists are sending the clones all over history to carry out their plan. At least they were, before their bootleg time-travel devices stopped working."

"What's the plan, though?" Sera asked.

"That's what we're here to find out." Riq gazed up the small staircase, toward the open doors. "Follow me," he said. "We need to see what's happening here."

Sera and Dak trailed Riq through the quiet halls of the school, peeking into empty classrooms as they walked.

"You've been here before?" Dak asked.

"Just last night," Riq said in a low voice. "I found a phony Dak wandering around seventeenth-century Rome, furious at being stranded." He gave Sera a rare smile. "Nice job ditching him, by the way. Anyway, he pretended to be the genuine article and asked me to bring him to this island on this date. I left him behind but decided to check out where his directions led. That's when I realized you two had been duped."

"In more ways than one," Dak said.

Riq gave him a blank look.

"I mean *duped* like *tricked* and *duped* like *duplicated*," Dak explained.

"Yeah," Riq said. "I got it. Language guy, remember?"

Sera grinned. She'd really missed how Riq handled Dak. "What else did you learn?" she asked.

"Not much," Riq said. "I got close enough to hear about the bogus Rings not working without you two, and that you'd both given them the slip. Then I got spotted and had to book it. In case you didn't notice, I don't really blend in here. I'm hoping having you with me will buy me some time. If anyone asks, I'll say I'm your uncle."

Dak shook his head. "Not sure that's gonna fly."

"So you don't know what they're being taught here?" Sera asked. "Are they learning how to be . . . us?"

"Dude, you can't *learn* to be me," Dak said. "You have to be born this way."

"They were born that way," Riq said. "They're identical to you in terms of IQ, height, weight, vision, hearing. . . ."

"But they're total jerks!" Dak countered.

Riq shrugged. "Maybe the SQ isn't training them to think like you. Maybe they're training the *yous* to think like *them*."

Right after Riq said this, a whistle wailed through the long hall. Sera spun around and saw a large older man in a gold-trimmed security uniform march toward them, spastically blowing his whistle.

"Come on!" Riq shouted, pulling Sera and Dak the other way. The three of them took off running. They rounded the near corner and sprinted a long stretch of hall and then ducked around a second corner.

"In here," Dak hissed, pointing toward a classroom door that was slightly ajar.

Sera followed the two boys into the classroom, where they found two Daks, approximately the same age as Dak was now, hovering over a model of Dak's actual house and barn back home.

The real Dak's eyes grew wide as he stared at the barn and then looked up at his clones. "Uh . . . hey," he said.

One of them stepped away from the model and gave Dak and Sera a head nod. "Mason hassling you guys about getting to class?"

"Yeah," Sera said, hoping she wouldn't give them away. "He's always . . . hassling people, isn't he?"

"Tell me about it," the other clone said, shaking his head. "We're stuck in this place, like, eight hours a day. Why can't we take a little time for ourselves here and there?"

Mason's whistle sounded closer.

"Cube of cheddar?" the other clone said, pulling a napkin out of his pocket.

The real Dak glanced at Sera and Riq before reaching his hand out. "Don't mind if I do, my good man." He popped a couple of cubes in his mouth and grinned while he chewed. "You guys are all right," he said with his mouth half full.

"So, what's up with this guy?" the first clone said, pointing at Riq. "He cool?"

"He's cool," Sera said.

"I'm cool," Riq agreed.

Mason was right outside the door now, shouting into his walkie-talkie, "I've got a possible code silver here. I repeat: code silver. Two sixth-grade versions on the run. No visible wristbands. Accompanied by an older boy who's not a student. Last seen heading west down Smyth Hall. Requesting backup."

The first clone opened a closet and said, "Get in! You don't want him to send you home."

Sera, Dak, and Riq squeezed into the closet, and the clone slid it closed. Sera stood beside Riq, trying not to make a sound, and listening. She heard the door open and Mason ask the clones if they'd seen anything out of the ordinary. They assured the man they hadn't, and Sera heard Mason leave and start blowing his whistle in the hall again.

"Thanks," Riq said to the clones as he stepped out of the closet. "Well, we should be going. I've gotta go tutor these two." He pulled Dak and Sera with him toward the door.

"Dude," one of the clones said to the other. "Doesn't he look like that language guy they taught us about last semester?"

"Oh yeah," the other one said. "The dope who used his genius to advance the Hystorian agenda and mess up this timeline."

"Dude," the real Dak said, "this is totally a clone of that dope."

Sera elbowed Dak in the ribs.

The two clones looked at each other. "A clone? Cool," one of them said.

"Yeah, sweet," the other one added. "Mad science."

Riq opened the door, and Sera and Dak followed him back out into the hall, where they looked both ways, but Mason was nowhere to be found. "Dude, this is getting a little creepy," Dak said.

"A *little*?" Sera said.

Dak shook his head. "Maybe wasting the day away in a hammock isn't such a bad idea after all. They should teach *that* here."

"Let's keep moving," Riq barked, and the three of them hurried back the other way.

"You're not a dope, by the way," Sera said as they continually passed empty classrooms.

"I've been called worse," Riq said. "I assumed part of the instruction here would be anti-Hystorian, and that confirmed it. They're being brainwashed."

In a few minutes, they came across a large lecture hall. They peeked through the window and saw that every seat was filled with Seras and Daks who looked to be a year or two older than Sera and Dak were now. Sera stared at another Sera through the window. She was taking notes in a notebook that looked exactly like the kind she used back in school.

"Come on," Riq said to Sera in a soft voice. He pointed down the hall, toward the back door of the lecture hall. They hurried over to it and Riq pulled it open slowly and quietly.

One Dak and two Seras turned to look at them, but

their presence wasn't causing that much of a stir. They huddled in the door and listened to the teacher.

". . . and tomorrow we'll look at the challenge of zero gravity," he was saying. "Tonight, I want you to read the first three chapters in your physics textbook."

Sera heard some of the people in the class moan. She realized it was just the Daks.

"Hey," the teacher said. "Nobody said this was going to be easy. Those self-righteous Hystorians messed up our timeline. We lost the Earth in a war with them. But we've set our sights on a much grander utopia now. And thanks to your brothers and sisters, we're close. We're so close, I can feel myself floating across the lunar surface."

Sera looked around the class as a buzz spread through all the students. Were they really setting their sights on space?

"That old man back in the cell we were in," Dak whispered, elbowing Sera, "didn't he say something about some lady taking over the 'heavens'?"

"Oh, man," Riq whispered. "He did."

"Is it possible he knows something?" Sera asked.

"I don't know how," Riq whispered. "But we should at least go back and talk to him. It sounds like these clones are getting close to something big."

Sera ushered them back out into the hallway. "They're not clones," she said.

Dak gave her a dirty look. "What else would they be?"

"Time is a river," Sera said. "Remember? And the Infinity Ring let us move up and down the river whenever we wanted."

"Go on," Riq said.

"But sometimes rivers branch off. A single river splits into two or three."

"What are you talking about?" Dak asked.

"I'm talking about alternate timelines. Parallel dimensions." Sera was so excited by the theoretical science, she almost tripped over her own words. "Weren't you listening? Those duplicates of yours mentioned *this* timeline. They didn't want to be sent home. They were surprised when you mentioned cloning."

"But how . . . ?" Riq began.

"I think Tilda's device isn't just a time-travel device," Sera said. "I think it's a dimensional-travel device. She needed a time-traveling army with our DNA, so she recruited versions of us from alternate realities. She fed them lies about what the Hystorians had done here. Told them they could save the world if they worked for her!"

Someone suddenly snatched Sera's arm from behind, barking, "Where are your ID bracelets?"

Sera spun around and found herself eye to eye with Mason, the security guard who'd been chasing them.

"Her dog ate them," Dak said.

"There are no dogs on the entire island," Mason shouted.

Dak cleared his throat. "I mean . . . her pet guinea pig?"

"Enough nonsense," Mason said. "I don't care what Tilda saw in you. We're sending you back to your own timeline. Plenty more where you came from."

"Now!" Riq shouted.

Sera ripped her arm out of Mason's grip and took off after Riq and Dak, back down the long hall.

"Get back here!" Mason shouted, racing after them.

They took a sharp turn and ran right out the front doors of the school and down the small staircase, onto the lawn.

Sera watched Dak accidentally slam right into another Dak who was coming back from lunch.

"Dude," the duplicate said, looking down at the sack lunch he'd dropped.

"Dude yourself," the real Dak answered.

And then something unexpected happened. The duplicate vanished into thin air.

"Whoa," Dak said.

"Let's get out of here," Riq said. "Come on, Dak."

Dak nodded and took Riq's arm.

Sera was still staring at the school, though. High above the doors, there was a line written in Latin that made her heart skip a beat: IN STATU QUO RES ERANT ANTE BELLUM.

"Riq," she said, pointing to it, "what does that say in English?"

Mason and two other guards were descending the steps now and closing fast.

"The state in which things were before the war," Riq told her. "Now grab on. We've got an old man to go speak to."

Sera grabbed on to Riq's other arm, and Riq tilted his head toward the bright blue sky and closed his eyes and started shaking.

The three guards were all blowing their whistles and waving for them to stop.

But Sera was stuck on that saying on the wall: *In statu quo res erant ante bellum*. The initials of two words made up *SQ*. And the initials of the last two words made up *AB*. Her stomach dropped out. She'd never really stopped to think about what either set of initials stood for. But there it was, clear as day.

In statu quo res erant ante bellum.

Or as Riq had just translated it: "The state in which things were before the war." Tilda's people weren't ready to admit defeat.

Sera didn't have time to break it down any further, though, because everything around her was now spinning furiously. And in a few seconds, she was enveloped in the darkness.

20

War of the Worlds

Riq was appalled by what he found back in Anatolia. His guards had taken it upon themselves to torture an inmate—when they knew full well that Riq believed torture was barbaric.

He, Dak, and Sera had come out of their warp just outside of the town prison he was in charge of, and while the rapid-fire warping seemed to be difficult on Dak and Sera, it hardly fazed Riq. Maybe his body had adjusted after all the warping he'd done over the past six weeks. Or maybe it had something to do with his skin absorbing the tachyon fluid. Whatever the case, while Dak and Sera sat there half dazed, trying to shake out the cobwebs, Riq hit the ground running.

Literally.

Before his shoes even made contact with the dirt, he was already hurrying toward the prison cell, eager to speak with the old man who he now believed might know something about Tilda and her so-called

AB Pacifists. But when he got to the end of the long hall, he found the prison cell completely empty. "Guards!" he shouted.

No one seemed to be around.

Riq knew something was happening. Something *big*. Tilda was close to pulling off the ultimate Break, which would change the course of history forever.

He slammed the heel of his hand against one of the bars. Yes, he'd made a new life in ancient Greece, but his heart would always be in the future. Sometimes, he felt like he cared about it more now than ever.

He sprinted from the jail over to his living quarters. "Guards!" he shouted as he pushed his way through the front doors. "Guards! I need to speak with you immediately!"

Still no answer.

And Sera's dog didn't come running when he whistled.

Where was everybody?

Riq was staring at his bedroom wall, trying to think, when he heard one of his horses whinnying in the distance. He headed straight for the field behind the house, and sure enough, there were all six of his guards.

And his missing prisoners, too.

They were all standing around, watching his most powerful horse drag the old man—who was wearing nothing but an undershirt and undershorts—all around the dusty field.

He couldn't believe they were torturing a man old enough to be their grandfather.

"Stop right this minute!" Riq shouted.

His guards spun around. So did the prisoners, and Riq saw that their hands were tied behind their backs. "Hephaestion!" his most loyal guard, Draco, called back. "You've returned early!"

"What in the name of Alexander the Great are you *doing* to this man?" Riq demanded.

"What's going on?" Dak called out as he and Sera approached from down the hill.

"Hephaestion," the second guard said. "This man cast away the animal you left in our care."

"Are you talking about my dog?" Sera shouted. She and Dak jogged the rest of the way, joining the guards and prisoners. "What happened to her?"

Riq lunged for the horse as it passed by in its circle, physically stopping it from dragging the old man. He untied the man's bloody wrists and feet and helped him up, saying, "This is an absolute travesty, sir. Are you okay?"

The old man's skin was all scratched up and covered in mud, and he was clearly dazed. Still, he managed to nod.

"Someone, get this man some water!" Riq shouted. "And his clothes! Now!"

One of the guards took off toward the prison quarters. Two of the other guards hurried over to the horse and led it away. The old man's ankles were badly swollen where the rope had chafed the skin.

Riq cringed and turned to Draco. "What is the meaning of this?"

"It's true what they said," Draco pleaded. "Believe me, Hephaestion. I took the dog with me while I did my rounds, and when we got to the prison cell, the old man put a spell on her. And as the gods are my witness, the dog vanished into thin air."

"It's true," one of the guards holding the rope said.

"He's an evil sorcerer," another guard said.

"She couldn't have just disappeared," Sera said. "She has to be somewhere."

"I saw it with my own eyes," Draco said.

Riq saw how upset Sera was, which made him feel even worse. It was his idea to leave the dog in the first place. "I assure you, Sera," he said, "we will find her."

She looked at the ground.

"One second, she was by my side," Draco said, "and then she was gone. I decided it was necessary to punish the old man until he brought back the dog using his witchcraft. I didn't want to disappoint you, sir."

One of the guards came running back with the old man's clothes and a cup of water. Riq helped the man dress and gave him the water. He dismissed all of his guards, ordering them to return the rest of the prisoners back to their cell. Then he had the old man, Dak, and Sera follow him back to his living quarters.

They sat in the chairs where only hours ago Riq had crowned Abdalonymus the king of Sidon. "What did you do to the girl's dog?" he asked, staring right into the old man's droopy eyes.

"Not a thing," the man answered. "But I'll tell you this. An animal does not vanish into thin air unless someone is altering the natural course of things."

"What's that supposed to mean?" Dak said.

The old man shook his head. He looked furious. "It's all part of her evil plan," he said, repeating the same words he'd been shouting from the minute he'd been taken into custody.

But Riq viewed them differently now.

"Whose plan?" Sera said. "Tilda?"

The man turned to her. "The woman with flaming red hair. The woman from the future."

It felt like someone had just punched Riq right in the gut. He was speaking about Tilda, of course, and had been all along. Why hadn't he listened to the old man earlier? "Where'd you meet her?" Riq asked him. "And what did she want?"

The old man touched his fingers around an especially large cut on his forehead. "She claimed that because of decisions made by those in power, the Earth was beginning to fall apart. If we agreed to join her group, going on a few select missions, she promised us a new kingdom in a place where the Earth's destruction couldn't touch us." The old man pointed up at the ceiling.

"Space," Riq said.

"Wait a second," Dak said. Riq could tell by the look on his face he was starting to put it together, too. "Guess why Fake Sera took me all the way back to ancient China!"

"They were the first to invent gunpowder!" Sera said.

"Right," Dak said. "She injected the man who actually invented gunpowder with some kind of memory-erasing drug and then took the chemicals he had combined to make gunpowder to a group of punks wearing golden robes. She wanted them to have gunpowder first."

"And *your* double took me back to the trial of Galileo," Sera said. "He had me defend Galileo's belief that the Earth revolved around the sun. The heliocentric theory. And guess who rigged the trial in my favor?"

"Someone from the AB," Dak said.

"Bingo." Sera looked at Riq. "One of the cardinals who ruled on the case was wearing a gold-trimmed robe."

"After China," Dak said, hopping up out of his chair, "your evil twin took me to Aunt Effie's farm in Massachusetts. What was happening there, you ask? Robert Goddard was testing the first liquid-fuel rocket . . . which led directly to modern-day space-travel technology."

"Don't you see what Tilda's doing?" Riq asked. The hair was standing up on the back of his neck.

Sera shot up out of her seat, too. "She may have conceded the Earth after we fixed all the Breaks," she said.

"But that doesn't mean she's given up. Now she's trying to colonize space."

"She's trying to colonize the *moon*," the old man corrected her. "And when she does, she told us she was going to initiate a war of the worlds."

Riq held up his hand to put the brakes on everyone's excitement. "You understand what you two've done, right?" he asked.

They all looked at him.

"You've unknowingly altered history," Riq said, "in *Tilda's* favor."

Riq watched Dak's and Sera's faces deflate, but the old man's expression didn't change at all. Riq studied him for a few long seconds before saying, "I'm curious — why didn't you follow Tilda when she promised you a new home in space? Sounds like a pretty good pitch to me."

The man's scratched-up face broke into a smile. "I was there when you three arrived in Greece. I saw the way Aristotle trusted you. I may have been born into a family of simple fishermen, but I always knew I was meant for something extraordinary, even as I got on in age. When I was approached by your woman with the flaming red hair, I realized what it was. I had to trek the twelve days it took to get here to issue my warning." He settled his gaze on Riq. "Thank you for finally listening. I was beginning to fear you didn't speak Greek at all."

PART FIVE

A Pebble between the Eyes

DAK MAY have wet his pants a little when he saw it.

He definitely screamed. Like, shrieked.

"Dak, outside!" Riq shouted.

But Dak was paralyzed with fear. They'd landed back in the present, in front of his house, only it no longer resembled the present he'd left only a short time ago. His barn had collapsed, and the forest was half scorched by fire, and there was a strange siren sound in the distance. But inside the house was worst of all. It looked ransacked, and his parents were nowhere to be found. Sera had dug up Dak's old digital encyclopedia, and they were looking up what historians had recorded about their actions in China and Rome and Massachusetts when suddenly they heard a deep growl behind their backs.

The three of them spun around and found a massive *Smilodon* cat sizing them up. Sera and Riq turned and ran, but Dak froze.

The ancient cat slobbered and growled at Dak again.

He and Sera had messed things up bad.

He was as scared as he'd ever felt in his life, but he was also fascinated. This giant cat was from the Pleistocene epoch, which ended over ten thousand years ago. But it started long before that, meaning the cat bearing down on him could be from two million years ago.

"Dak, run!" Sera screamed.

When a huge paw took a swipe at him, that's exactly what Dak did. He turned and ran, following Sera and Riq out of the house. "There's a ladder out back!" Dak shouted.

They raced around the side of the house and flew up the ladder to the top of the house. They huddled together on the slanted roof, the *Smilodon* cat roaring at them from below.

"What do we do?" Sera said.

"Nothing," Riq said. "Except wait."

Dak scoffed. "Doesn't look like it's going anywhere soon."

"Let's at least pull out Dak's encyclopedia," Sera said. "Obviously, it's even worse than we thought. I guess you weren't lying about that pterosaur, Dak."

"Or hallucinating," Dak said, staring down at the enraged animal. It seemed content to pace for now, but if it decided to leap, they might still be in big trouble. Dak shifted his attention to his barn. Or what was *left* of his barn. The whole thing had collapsed somehow.

His hammock was lying on the ground, useless. It didn't seem like a good sign that his parents were gone and a *Smilodon* cat had moved in.

"The old man was telling the truth," Riq said. "It says here that after successfully disproving the geocentric theory, Galileo became a celebrity — and a party animal. He never produced any more ideas."

"That's terrible!" Sera said. "He was supposed to publish a book in 1638. One of the most important books in the history of physics."

"There's nothing about that here," Riq said. "And get this: Gunpowder was invented by the Pacifists. It took the rest of the world another half century to figure it out."

"So what now?" Dak said.

"We have to go back and fix your mistakes," Riq said. "And to be as efficient as possible, we're going to have to separate."

The three of them had warped from Anatolia to the present to see how the new Breaks — which Dak and Sera had helped create — were affecting present-day life. But Dak had never expected *this.* He saw that his mom's campaign signs had been pulled up and trampled.

Where were his parents?

"We all have time-traveling devices," Riq said. "So it should be fine . . . though obviously we'll be on our own."

"I guess Dak and I can go fix the Breaks we were there for," Sera said. "But what about you?"

"Russia," Riq answered.

"Russia?"

"If this is about a race to the moon," Riq said, "then it's going to involve America and Russia. Right, Dak?"

Dak turned to look at Riq. "Yeah, America and Russia."

Sera shook Dak by the arm. "That's your cue to launch into some big rant about the space race. You know, there was that Soviet rocket scientist Sergei . . ."

"Korolev," Dak said, distracted. "The father of practical aeronautics."

Sera waited for him to say more, and when he didn't, she tried to goad him into it. "Oh, yeah, and because of him, weren't the Soviets the first to launch a satellite into orbit? And then they sent an animal into space, I think. A dog. What was its name again?"

"Laika," he said.

"Exactly!" She stared expectantly at Dak for a few long seconds, but he wasn't in the mood. He was too worried about his parents. And his barn. And everything else that seemed to be messed up in the present because of what he and Sera had done. Oh, and there was also the fact that a five-hundred-pound cat wanted to eat them for lunch.

"Don't you get it?" he said. "This is bigger than the Breaks. History is *shattered*. And this time, it's all our fault."

"Hey," Sera said, elbowing Dak in the arm. "It's going to be okay. This isn't our first rodeo."

Suddenly, a huge pterosaur emerged from the trees. Dak was almost blown off the roof when it flew over them, flapping its massive wings. It squawked so loudly, it rattled Dak's eardrums. He turned back to Sera. "Yeah, we've so got this," he said sarcastically.

"Hey, cat!" someone shouted from nearby.

Dak scanned the yard from his perch. He spotted Arin, hiding behind a tree, whistling to try to divert the massive cat's attention. She looked up at Dak, Sera, and Riq and said, "These things are all over the forest now. I'm almost too afraid to cross through it now. *Almost.*"

"Arin!" Riq called out.

She looked up at him. "How do you know my name?"

"I don't," Riq said. "I just . . . Dak here told me."

"Dak?" Arin didn't know him either. He watched the girl shrug and pull a slingshot out of her satchel. "Let's see if I can't get it off your case."

She took aim and shouted, "Hey!" When the *Smilodon* cat turned around, she fired a small rock that cracked the animal right between the eyes. It ducked its head and immediately took off out of the yard, back into the forest.

Dak climbed back down the ladder, followed by Sera and Riq. "Nice shot," he said.

She shrugged. "I do what I have to do to survive in this crazy world."

Dak looked at her for a while, waiting for some sign of recognition. "You don't remember me?" he asked.

She shook her head. "Why would I?"

"Guys," Sera said, "we should really go. Like, now." She turned to Arin and said, "Thanks so much for what you did. We were afraid we might be there all day, and we have some urgent business to tend to."

"Oh, don't let me keep you," Arin said. She picked up her stack of books from the ground, and Dak tried to see what she had. It wasn't vampires this time, it was a bunch of dystopian novels—which made sense, considering she seemed to be living in a dystopian world. Or was it apocalyptic? He could never remember the difference between the two.

"Did you guys see that dinosaur fly over the forest just now?" Arin asked.

They all nodded.

"Well, technically," Dak pointed out, "what we just saw was a pterosaur, but . . ."

Arin looked at him like he was crazy.

Well, it was nice that some things didn't change.

"Can you tell us what's been happening here?" Riq asked.

Arin glanced at Dak's fallen barn and said, "Some really freaky things. They've been happening all over the world, actually. Ancient pirate ships have been spotted off the coasts. Dinosaurs—the *real* kind—have been walking down highways in the middle of the day." She pointed toward Dak's barn. "This place was actually trampled by a sauropod, which, I don't know if you know this—"

"It's the largest dinosaur that ever lived," Dak said, finishing her sentence. "That's what happened to my parents' barn? A *dinosaur* stepped on it?"

"Guys, we should really fix these Breaks right away," Sera said. "Something tells me we don't have a lot of time."

"Do you have any idea where my parents could have gone?" Dak asked Arin. "They lived here."

"A lot of people drove toward the mountains or are hiding out in bomb shelters." Arin looked to Sera. "Where are you guys going anyway? Maybe I can help."

"You can," Riq said. "Tell us what you know about current space travel. We were looking through the encyclopedia, but we can't find any information."

"The Pacifists are pretty secretive," Arin said, "but stuff leaks."

"Any information you can give us would be a help," Dak said.

"You know how the Pacifists established a colony on the moon in the nineties?" Arin said. When there was no recognition on any of their faces, she said, "Wait, you don't even know about *that*? Have you been living under a rock?"

"Something like that," Riq said.

"Okay, I'll give you the CliffsNotes version," Arin said. "The Pacifists have been living up there for over a year now, while their scientists try to create a permanent atmosphere. And it turns out they're not as into peace as their name suggests. It's just been reported that they've built nuclear weapons up there, and they're threatening to wipe out everyone on Earth if they don't get what they want."

"And what do they want?" Riq asked.

"Absolute power."

Dak looked up at the sky. It was still sunny out, so he couldn't see the moon, but the thought of a nuke launching toward the Earth from space was almost incomprehensible. It snapped him out of his mood. Yes, his parents were gone—*again*—and he had no idea where they were, but the situation was dire for everyone, not just him. "Guys," he said to Sera and Riq, "we need to do this *now*."

"Thanks for your help," Riq said to Arin.

"Wait. I have one last question," Sera said. "Where are these Pacifists sending up their spacecraft from?"

"I heard it was some island in Europe," Arin said. "Though nobody knows for sure. Like I said, they're very secretive for security purposes."

Sera looked at Dak and Riq. "Santorini. Should we agree to meet there on a certain day?"

Riq did a quick search on Dak's digital encyclopedia. In a few seconds, he looked up and said, "July 16, 1969. Hey, isn't that when America first put a man on the moon?"

Dak's eyes lit up. "Yeah! The one small step didn't happen until July 20. But the launch itself was July 16."

"What are you talking about?" Arin said. "America has never put a man on the moon. Nobody else has. That's why everyone marvels at the Pacifists. There's a reason their rockets are lined with gold, or so the joke goes."

Dak shook his head, remembering all the Dak and Sera duplicates they'd seen on Santorini. He wondered how many had ended up on the moon. Maybe that had something to do with his dream about being in space.

After a long stretch of silence, Arin said, "Okay, I guess I'll leave you to it, then."

Dak watched her walk away. She seemed to genuinely want to help, and he wondered if they could have included her more somehow. He turned back to Sera and Riq, who were already preparing for their respective warps. Sera was programming her Ring, and Riq was staring at his arm and taking these weird, deep yoga breaths.

"Are we ready, then?" Sera said.

Riq nodded.

"I still don't understand how you can warp without a Ring," Dak said.

"That makes two of us," Riq answered.

They both turned to Sera, the science whiz, but all she did was shrug.

"Anyway," Riq said. "I guess it's time. Good luck to you guys."

"Good luck," Dak and Sera both said at the same time.

Dak programmed his own Ring.

They looked at one another for several seconds, like they didn't want to split up now that they were finally back together. "I'm sorry I doubted you," Dak told Sera.

"It's my fault," Sera responded. "I knew it couldn't be the real you."

Now that they were going to split up again, Dak felt his heart swell. The three of them just stared at one another for a few long seconds. Then they laughed a little, even with everything hanging over their heads. These two were like family to him now.

Sera was the first one to hit her ACTIVATE button, and in seconds she disappeared.

Riq was next. He tilted his head back and closed his eyes, and his whole body began trembling. Then, *poof*, he was gone, too.

Dak looked at his fallen barn one more time. His house, which no longer held his parents. And then he stared at the half-torched forest. Finally, he hit the ACTIVATE button, and the world around him began to spin — though he now knew, from watching Sera and Riq warp away without him, that the spinning happened only on the inside. The last thing Dak saw before he closed his eyes and gave himself to the warp was Arin, who was once again hiding behind a tree on his parents' property, watching him.

And then he was gone.

2 2

Separate but Equal

SERA LANDED in seventeenth-century Rome, right before the trial of Galileo. She hurried up to the doors of the courtroom where she saw herself and Dak trying to get in, and the guards who barred their way.

She experienced something beyond déjà vu.

It was impossible to describe what it was like to see herself there, with Dak, looking so uncertain. She had been so naïve in that moment. But at least she'd had her no-name dog. She missed her so much. Maybe she could fix the Break she had created *and* get her dog back.

But first she had to concentrate on fixing her mistake.

She watched the group of AB Pacifists step up to the guards and talk to them in quiet voices, and then the guards stepped aside, letting Dak and Sera into the courtroom where Sera would testify on Galileo's behalf. Sera followed herself inside, looking for her opportunity to replace this earlier version of herself. And then she remembered how light-headed she'd felt before getting

Dak's translation device. Her body had been fighting off the effects of the tamales. That was her opening.

She followed closely behind them, and she saw herself falter and go down on one knee, just as she remembered. Sera darted forward and touched her dupicate lightly on the ankle. Her previous self disintegrated into thin air. And so did her dog. It happened in an instant.

Sera had expected the other version of herself to fade out, just like what had happened to Dak's duplicate at the school. Everything she knew about quantum theory suggested that the time stream hated a paradox. Two versions of the same person were not supposed to be in the same place at the same time. Given the chance, time would fix itself. But as long as she had a Ring on her, she could stay right where she was. Or *when* she was.

The dog was another matter. Why had she faded out again? Sera was beginning to suspect someone else's hand at work there.

One second they were there, the next they were gone.

There was no time to wonder about it, though, because right at that second Dak spun around, ready to swap his translation device into her ear, except she wasn't right behind him like he expected.

"Sera?" he called out.

Sera ripped out her own translation device, shoved it in her pocket, and sprinted over to him, saying, "I'm right here." The dog sniffed her suspiciously, but seemed content. Sera smelled like Sera despite the swap.

"Come on," Dak said anxiously. "They're just about to

issue their verdict." He stopped her near the back row of chairs and transferred the translation device from his ear into Sera's—which was still gross—just as one of the cardinals slammed his gavel against the table.

"We have our verdict," the man announced.

Everything was happening just like she remembered it. Only now she understood what the outcome of her defense would be. Galileo, this man who was her idol, who had advanced science in so many profound ways, would turn his back on his work because of his new-found popularity. She looked at him now.

She had to save him by *not* saving him.

"By majority vote," the cardinal went on, "we find the defendant, Galileo Galilei—"

"Wait!" Dak said, leaping out from behind the last row of chairs. Everyone spun around to look at him. "My friend here, Sera Froste . . . she has something to say. Right, Sera?"

The fake Dak leaned in close to her and said, "What are you waiting for? Do it now."

The man pounded his gavel again and said, "The court does not appreciate interruptions such as this. Guards, have them removed immediately."

"Let her have her say," the cardinal with the gold-trimmed robe called out. "We must have all evidence in order to make the proper decision."

The first cardinal turned to Sera, clearly angry, and said, "Well?"

Could Sera really do this? Could she give incorrect

testimony in order to make sure Galileo was punished? Because that was what she'd have to do in order to keep him on track to becoming the scientific giant he was supposed to become. But could she really lie in court?

Sera stepped forward and announced, "Galileo is wrong about the heliocentric theory, and I can prove it!"

There was a buzz in the courtroom.

The cardinal in the gold-trimmed robe stepped up and said, "Throw her out of court immediately! She has no right to speak!"

The other cardinals disagreed, though. "Let the girl speak!" one of them insisted.

"She should be allowed to have her say," said another. "Just like you pointed out a second ago."

The first cardinal pounded his gavel especially hard to quiet the crowd. "The floor is yours, young woman, but be quick about it."

Sera took a deep breath and let it out slow. She looked at Galileo, then at her dog. Then she turned back to the cardinals and began speaking out against her idol.

Riq was no history buff, but something he read in Dak's electronic encyclopedia had really struck him. According to the section he read about the space race, the USSR had never accomplished much. The encyclopedia entry said that they were making progress at first, along with

America and the AB Pacifists, until a particular launch went horribly wrong. They had tried launching a dog named Laika into space in an attempt to determine whether space travel was safe for living things. But Laika's spacecraft exploded into a million pieces long before it left Earth's atmosphere, and the entire Russian space program was dismantled as a result. According to the encyclopedia entry, Russia's top scientists and rocket engineers were ordered to never look toward space again.

But Riq knew this was all wrong. He didn't know how the Pacifists had rigged it, but he knew he had to warp back to the launch of that dog. He trusted that he'd be able to figure out *something*.

He landed as close to the launch site as he dared. Even if he didn't have Pacifists to worry about, Soviet security was bound to be intense. He had to be ready for anything.

What he wasn't ready for was the dog. It came out of nowhere: a cute, energetic mutt running straight for him. Before he could react, the dog ran circles around him, sniffing at his feet and yipping excitedly.

It was the same dog his men had managed to lose in Anatolia. "What in the world are you doing here?" he said.

"She's with us," a woman's voice answered.

Riq tensed. The dog ran away from him and heeled beside an older couple, a man and a woman with smatterings of gray in their jet-black hair.

The man smiled. "Riq, right?"

Riq pointed at himself. "Me? Yeah, I'm Riq. Who are you?"

This time the woman spoke up. "We're Sera Froste's parents."

Riq's stomach dropped. He didn't know much about these people, but from what he'd gathered, they couldn't be trusted. He scanned their outfits for gold, but saw none.

"Don't worry," Sera's father said. "Everything's taken care of here. The launch will go as planned and the Soviet space program will proceed."

"Well, with one small alteration," Sera's mother said, patting the dog on the head.

"And I'm supposed to just take your word for it?" Riq said.

"We're on your side, Riq," Mr. Froste said. "Tilda came to us. She wanted to blackmail us into helping her rebuild her empire. But we saw an opportunity to thwart her plans from the inside."

"We let our daughter believe we had crossed back over to the SQ," Mrs. Froste added. "We had to do it. To protect her."

"To *protect* her?" Riq said. "Do you know what she's doing right now? She's warping through time, risking her life. Again!"

Mr. Froste lowered his head, like this hit him hard.

"Our little girl is quite capable," Mrs. Froste said. "So

capable that we had to sabotage her experiments until everything was in place."

Riq shot daggers at her. "I can't believe you put her through all that. Your daughter is the smartest, most loyal person I've ever met. But you wouldn't know that because you're never around. And you let her think you were actually her enemies? That you didn't care about her?"

"She's the only thing we care about," Mrs. Froste countered. "How do you think Tilda got to us in the first place? She threatened Sera. She said she could get to her any time. Even find her as a baby in her crib."

Riq's anger faltered.

"We've done the best we could," Mr. Froste said, "with a bad situation. When Tilda forced us to reproduce the Infinity Ring, we made sure the DNA lock remained in place. When she worked around that by pulling alternate versions of the kids from branches of the time stream, we sabotaged her by making it so that the Rings could tell the difference between the real Sera, the real Dak, and the alternates."

"Think of it as temporal DNA," Mrs. Froste said. "Those duplicates have the same genes as the kids, but their chronal signatures are totally different."

"If you say so," Riq said. It was a lot to swallow.

"But that's not the best part," she added. "Riq, you're our secret weapon."

"Me?" he said.

"Let me ask you a question," Sera's mom said. "Don't you think it's odd that you're able to warp around through time without an Infinity Ring?"

"It's because I splashed tachyon fluid all over myself," Riq said.

Sera's dad shook his head. "That alone wouldn't get you anywhere. That's the fuel, but it's useless without an engine. But we knew we could trust you to undermine Tilda and keep her busy while we made our move."

"So we found you in Greece when you were asleep one night," his wife said. She pointed at Riq's shoulder. "And we planted a microchip in your arm that would allow you to warp anywhere at any time."

"Including the twenty-first century," Mr. Froste said. "You can go home again, Riq."

Riq remembered the inexplicable scar on his right shoulder. He realized he'd just visited the future, messed up though it was, and hadn't suffered any ill effects. Maybe they were telling the truth. He watched as the dog sniffed around a fence a few yards away. "And you abducted Sera's dog because . . . ?"

"We're the ones who left the dog for her in the first place," the woman explained, pulling a small silver device from her pocket. "Watch this. Here, girl!" She pressed a button on the device and the dog vanished, reappearing a moment later at Mrs. Froste's feet.

"Quantum leash," she said. "For the Soviet space program to continue as it's meant to, this dog has to go up in that ship. But there's no reason she has to die up there."

"You were right about one thing, Riq" Sera's dad said. "We weren't there for our daughter. And we owe you more than we can say for standing by her through all of this."

"But if we beat Tilda once and for all, we can finally be the parents she deserves," Mrs. Froste said. "What do you say?"

Riq only hesitated for a moment. Then he broke out into a smile. "I say let's do this. For Sera. And everybody else."

Dak stopped to watch the men meditating in the Buddhist temple in ancient China. He wondered if they'd ever defeat Tilda once and for all. Because this seemed like a better, more peaceful way to live. Imagine if everyone had inner peace. Not just the people who entered temples like this. He then walked through the entrance of the dark and dingy warehouse for a second time.

A flood of images jockeyed for position in his brain as he moved through the long hallway. The alchemist. The boy with the birthmark. The bad piece of Gouda. When he approached the door to the alchemist's workshop, he saw the boy standing there with a less-informed version of himself. Now it seemed idiotic to him that he hadn't known he was trying to track down a fake Sera. But at the time he'd genuinely thought it was his best friend.

He looked over the shoulder of the boy and the naïve

Dak and saw, once again, the alchemist add a chemical to a small bowl made of stone, which resulted in a minor explosion that made the old man and fake Sera leap back from the workbench. The man spoke excitedly, and this time, Dak could understand him.

This man had just discovered the chemical composition of gunpowder, which would change the world forever. Except the fake Sera wanted the AB Pacifists to have that technology first. Dak wouldn't let that happen.

He reached out and tapped his younger self on the shoulder, ready to make his move. But it turned out he didn't have to do much. He watched in shock as the other version of himself disintegrated into thin air. Dak stood there, eyes bugging out of his head, until he noticed the boy bringing the piece of Gouda up to his mouth. That's when Dak sprang into action.

He reached for the kid and knocked the cheese out of his hand, saying, "Don't eat that; it's poisoned." The boy gave him a strange look but after a few seconds he nodded, and Dak knew the translation device was doing its job.

When Dak turned his attention back to the workshop, he saw Sera pulling out her syringe and aiming it at her victim's neck. Dak ran toward them and dove through the air, tackling Sera's duplicate just before the needle penetrated the old man's flesh. The syringe crashed to the ground and rolled to the wall, useless.

Dak and Sera tumbled to the ground together, and Dak

rolled on top of her and pinned her arms. Sera looked up at him and shouted, "What are you doing, Dak?"

"Making things right," he told her.

He motioned to the boy. "Bring me the rope from the shelf by your feet. Hurry."

The boy came with the rope, and together they tied up the fake Sera's arms and legs, and Dak stood up.

"You'll never get away with this," she told him. Although she was tied up so thoroughly that she couldn't even move her hands and feet, a smile came over her face. "There are thousands more just like me. And we will win. And when we win, you will pay."

"We'll see about that," Dak said. Then he turned his attention back to the boy. "Get this man to safety. I will take care of the girl."

He watched the boy take the alchemist by the arm and start leading him away. He looked at Sera, whose eyes were furious. With her detained in China, Robert Goddard would be safe in Massachusetts.

That meant they had only one task left. But it was a big one.

Prelaunch

"Well, this is a new one," Sera said. She and Dak were standing outside the towering barbwire fence that protected the AB Pacifists' launch site.

"What do you mean?" Dak said.

Sera motioned toward her gear from seventeenth-century Rome. "Usually, we're trying to find clothes that make us look like everyone else," she said. "This time, Riq's out there trying to find us clothes that'll make us look like . . . us."

Dak glanced down at his robe from ancient China. "I just hope he hurries. It looks like these Pacifist dudes are close to getting started."

The first part of their plan had worked perfectly. The three of them had fixed their respective Breaks — separately — and then successfully warped to Santorini, on July 16, 1969. Now for the most important part: stopping the Pacifists from getting to the moon.

Through the fence, Sera watched several dozen Dak

and Sera dupes milling around, doing checks on their spacecraft, and observing the weather and transporting supplies into the cockpit and fueling the engine. Sera knew what was at stake. They all did. Even with the other Breaks fixed, if they let this vessel get into orbit, Tilda would colonize the moon with her Pacifists, and once their settlement was up and running, they would turn their attention toward the Earth.

"I still can't believe we doubted each other," Dak said, looking at Sera. "Never again, okay?"

"Never again," Sera agreed. It was still strange to hear Dak being so . . . nice. She remembered the fake Dak apologizing to her back home. But this time was different. She knew it was really him, and it meant so much. "I have to admit something," she told him. "I've never felt so alone as when I thought I'd lost my best friend."

"It was the same for me," Dak said.

"Let's not start patting one another on the back just yet, okay?" Riq said, walking up behind them. He tossed them each some clothes and stepped up to the fence. "We still have to make sure we can get you two inside this fortress."

It didn't matter how many times Sera came to this island; she didn't think she'd ever get used to how weird it was watching so many people who looked just like her running around. People who *were* just like her, probably, before Tilda had gotten her claws into them. It saddened her to think of it: infinite possibilities, and so many of them ruined by one woman.

"So when are you going to fill us in on this plan of yours? Dak asked Riq.

"On the way to the portables."

"Portables?" Dak said. "As in . . . portable bathrooms? I think I'll pass, thanks."

"Just come on," Riq said.

Sera shrugged and followed Riq.

Dak did, too. Reluctantly.

Sera put on the clothes Riq had given her and studied herself in the tiny portable-bathroom mirror. She looked just like herself, which meant she looked like every other Sera cruising around on the entire island. Even though technically it was 1969, the Daks and Seras were all from the twenty-first century, and they all had scarily identical fashion sense.

Sera left her clothes from Rome on top of the toilet and left her portable. On her way to meet up with the two boys, she reviewed her part of Riq's plan. She and Dak were going to try and get past security by pretending to be technicians. Once they got inside, they were going to split up. Again. Her job was to talk her way into the control center. Dak was the one who had the more dangerous job. He was going to try and get onto the actual spacecraft.

"You ready?" Riq asked when Sera caught up to them.

"Ready as I'll ever be," she said.

"And you?" he said to Dak.

"One day, you'll figure this out about me, big guy," Dak answered. "I'm always ready when it comes to saving the world."

"That's what I like to hear," Riq said. "Okay, the security checkpoint is about a hundred yards to my left. Remember what I said: As long as you act like you know what you're doing, people will assume you belong. Obviously you both look the part. But you'll have to hurry. There's not much time."

Dak and Sera barely spoke on the long walk to the security checkpoint. For Sera, it was nerves. She knew this was probably the most ambitious thing they'd ever tried to do. It wasn't every day you tried to hijack a space mission. But she was also nervous for Dak. She had faith in him, and he'd grown a lot since they'd linked up with the Hystorians. But this was one tough job Riq had assigned to him.

Then again, they were going to war. And Riq had experience *winning* wars. She had faith in him, too.

Sera pulled the wristband out of her jeans when the checkpoint was only about a hundred feet away. She slipped it on and said, "Ready?"

She watched Dak slip his wristband on, too. "Ready," he said.

But he looked scared. And that made Sera scared. She grabbed him by the arm and stopped him. "Hey," she said. "You okay? I'll be right there in the control center, watching everything."

"Eight minutes until launch!" a woman's voice said over the loudspeaker. "Positions!"

"I know you will," Dak said.

They walked up to the checkpoint, making small talk, and tried to walk right through.

"Excuse me?" an older version of Sera said. "Wristbands?"

"Oh, sorry," Sera said, moving her arm toward the teen girl.

The girl checked her wrist and rolled her eyes. "You should know better than to try and just walk through a checkpoint."

"I totally wasn't thinking," Sera said.

"Obviously," the girl said, looking at Dak's wristband. "You should surprise us all and try it sometime."

Sera grinned through the whole exchange, even though she really wanted to give the teen version of herself a piece of her mind. But what did it matter? The girl waved them through the gate. And that's all they really wanted. The wristbands Riq scored for them were legit.

They found themselves surrounded by dozens of duplicates, maybe hundreds, all of them rushing around doing some job. All of them pulled from their homes, their realities, by Tilda. It was surreal. Sera couldn't believe how much things had changed from their first warp.

But there was one thing Dak, Sera, and the AB all had in common. They liked order. The movement of the crowd wasn't as chaotic as it appeared. Everyone had a task. Everything was labeled. And signs led the real Dak and Sera to the ready room, where they easily overpowered a Dak dupe as he suited up for space travel.

Dak took the gear for himself as his double vanished, returning home.

"Five minutes until launch!" the announcer said. Something about the voice made Sera's skin crawl.

"If I die up there," Dak said, "you can have my hammock."

"You're not gonna die, Dak." Sera patted him on the shoulder awkwardly. "You're like a roach. Nothing can kill you."

"Oh, great. Thanks."

"You know what I mean," Sera said. "Seriously, though, be careful."

Dak nodded. "You'll be able to make it to the control room yourself?"

"Oh, yeah," Sera said. "You can count on me."

"I know," he said.

He started to leave when Sera said, "And, Dak?"

He turned around to face her.

"I really do feel lucky to have you as a best friend."

A small smile broke on Dak's face. "Thanks."

A whole sea of butterflies started flapping around in Sera's stomach as she watched Dak hurry out of the room. Not because their mission depended on what happened next. But because Sera wanted more than anything for Dak to be okay.

Sera made her way quickly and quietly to the control room. It was set up like a NASA control center she'd seen in movies. In fact, it reminded her a little bit of the Hystorian Operations Center, where she'd first met Riq and Arin way back when this had all begun.

She wasn't surprised to find the room populated with versions of herself. After all, if you had to put either Dak or her in front of a computer, she was the obvious choice.

What did surprise her was the woman at the very center of the room, overlooking the entire operation. The woman was old. Very old. And frail-looking. She sat hunched in a wheelchair. She had plastic tubes running fluids into her arm.

Sera might have assumed she was getting a glimpse of herself in old age. But there was no mistaking the hate burning in the woman's cloudy eyes. Or the shade of red she'd used to dye the very tips of her stringy white hair.

It was Tilda. And she had to be a hundred years old.

"Commence countdown!" she barked, and her raspy voice was broadcast across the base. "Ten! Nine . . ."

Sera had expected a fight. She had expected to face Tilda one last time in heated battle. But this woman had already lost. She'd spent her entire life warping back and forth through time and across dimensions, manipulating everyone she came in contact with. She'd been consumed with hatred and jealousy and master plans. And now all she had left was a final, desperate gambit to control Earth's future by controlling the moon.

Sera felt pity for the woman, but there was no way she would sit back and let that happen.

The spacecraft's engine began to roar as Tilda counted down. When she reached zero, there was a sound of explosions as huge balls of fire flared from beneath the ship. Sera knew the solid rocket booster had ignited. She knew she was witnessing the almost-miraculous result of millennia of human progress. She felt a sense of wonder at how many little moments in history had all led to this one great moment.

Her heart climbed into her throat as the spacecraft launched into the air, speeding toward space.

"Good luck, Dak," she said.

And then she leisurely strolled up to a control panel, right under the nose of her greatest enemy, and steered her best friend's spacecraft into the path of an oncoming asteroid.

24

Trip to the Moon

THE HEAT from the fire was unbearable as Dak tried to claw his way out of the elaborate seat belt. Sweat streamed down his face. It soaked his shirt and pants underneath his bulky suit. It even soaked the protective diaper he'd been forced to wear by the Pacifist space authority—which turned out to be an ideal hiding place for the golden Infinity Ring. It was the diaper that triggered his memory. Dak realized this was exactly like the dream he'd had while he was safe in his hammock.

It had been a Remnant of a sort. A glimpse of things that could or would or should happen. A sign that history had been manipulated again. That it was breaking.

But this time, he was happy for it. Because he knew almost everything that was going to happen before it happened.

He knew when he glanced at the fire, it would be inching closer to the control panel, which meant it was inching closer to him.

He needed to get out of the way *now*!

He knew the fire had started when a few exposed fan wires shorted, igniting the Teflon insulation in the pure oxygen environment. But he now also knew the fire caught because he'd started it. It was all part of their plan.

"Come on!" Dak shouted, like he knew he would, as the belt slipped out of his sweaty fingers again. A drop of sweat ran into his right eye, momentarily blurring his vision. He blinked away the stinging sensation, knowing that when he looked to his left, he'd find two other astronauts—both Dak clones only a year or two older than him—peering out the window, screaming like little babies. "Uh, little help over here?" Dak shouted.

But he knew they wouldn't even turn around.

He heard a low buzzing sound, barely audible over the screams, and unlike in his dream, this time he knew it was one of those flying SQuares that the Pacifists had used to spy on him and Sera. He didn't see where it was, but it didn't matter. There wasn't going to be anything salvageable anyway.

When Dak was finally able to free himself, he drifted awkwardly out of the cockpit, toward the wall with the fire extinguisher. He snatched it in his gloves, removed the safety, and aimed the nozzle at the angry blue flame, which now claimed almost a third of the cockpit. But now he knew that this was all for show. The other Dak astronauts turned and saw him trying to put out the fire, and that was all that mattered.

The older duplicates started screaming even louder,

this time diving toward the center of the cockpit, near the fire, holding on to each other. Dak chucked the extinguisher to the side and bounded over to the window to see for himself.

And suddenly he was screaming, too.

Because even though he knew what he would find, it was still insane to see a massive asteroid, more than twice the size of their vessel, spinning recklessly through space directly toward them.

Instead of panicking, Dak locked the manual controls. Once he was sure there was going to be a collision, he pulled his golden Infinity Ring out of his diaper and programmed it to the present. He was just about to hit the ACTIVATE button when he looked at the two older Daks. They weren't on his side, but he couldn't just leave them.

He leapt through the growing fire and slapped them on the backs of their heads. They were gone in an instant and an eerie silence descended in the moment before impact.

The asteroid slammed into the Pacifist spacecraft just as the one true Dak Symth was sucked back into the warp.

Homecoming

A WEEK later, Riq was finally able to return to the present for good. He walked leisurely toward Dak's place, enjoying the nice weather and the total absence of bloodthirsty warriors. It was a pleasant change.

After Dak had warped back from outer space in one piece and they had judged their mission a success, Riq had gone directly back to Anatolia to tie up some loose ends. He was finally able to release the remainder of his war prisoners, whom he personally led back into the heart of Persia. He also awarded the old man who'd informed him about Tilda's plan a place in Alexander the Great's cabinet. And then he had a long talk with Alexander himself, about his plan to leave the era for good. He was worried that his friend would be disappointed, but Alexander only patted him on the back and said, "Go and do what makes you happy, Hephaestion."

Riq felt nostalgic now, realizing he'd never be called by that name again.

But that wasn't all he had taken care of in the time since they'd thwarted the plan to colonize the moon. He also made one final trip to Izamal, where he broke every Hystorian rule in the book.

He spoke to Kisa. He had to. It wasn't a long conversation, and he didn't give away too much about the future, but he did reveal that she was the reason he had chosen to go home. He wanted to find whatever family he had left in the present and build a life with them. Because when he was in Izamal he had learned that it isn't enough to simply commit yourself to a cause. In order to appreciate how truly wonderful a life on this Earth is, you must also know love. He told her that *she* had taught him that. They hugged briefly and then Riq said his good-byes.

Of course, he was never going to mention that detour to Dak, whom he now spotted lying in some sort of hammock outside his house. Sera was there, too, sitting on the grass, petting her dog. He was excited to see them again and called out, "Long time, no see!"

Dak and Sera both looked up and said, "Riq!"

"We were just talking about you," Sera said.

Riq gave Sera a quick hug and slapped hands with Dak. He sat down on the grass next to Sera and her dog.

"All that time I had no idea what her name was," Sera said. "Watch this. Laika, come give momma some love!"

Riq watched the dog jump on Sera and start licking her face over and over. Sera was laughing and pushing her away, but Riq could tell Sera loved every second of it. "So, you asked your parents for a pet and they got you the famous Soviet space dog?"

"She's the best dog in history," Sera said. "I'm so glad they were able to save her without causing a Break."

"They're suckers for animals, just like Sera," Dak added. "They said they couldn't let a dog get hurt in the name of science."

"So, everything's okay with them?" Riq asked.

"Everything's great," Sera said.

"They're like the model family of the year," Dak said.

Riq smiled, marveling at the foresight of Sera's parents. He touched his shoulder where they'd installed the microchip that allowed him to warp around through time. He made a mental note to thank them in person before he began searching for any long-lost family members of his own.

"And everything seems to be normal again in the present?" Riq asked.

"So far, so good," Sera said. "No dinosaur sightings yet."

"*Or* pterosaur sightings," Dak put in.

Sera rolled her eyes. "Exactly. I only worry that Dak's going to get bored again."

"No way," Dak said. "I learned my lesson. I'm content to hang out. With my friends." He looked directly at Riq. "We're so glad you're back here, man. Even though you are kind of a pain sometimes."

"Yeah," Sera said. "I mean, I'm glad you're here. Not the part about you being a pain."

The three of them got quiet for a few seconds after that. Riq cleared his throat, about to tell them his plans for the future, when he heard the voice of a girl behind him.

"Excuse me?" It was Arin, standing at the bottom of the driveway. "Does anyone know where I can find a Mr. and Mrs. Froste?"

Riq and Dak looked at Sera who said, "Uh, yeah. Why?"

"They told me to meet them here this afternoon. Apparently they want to discuss a job. Something that could 'really make history.' Their words."

Riq saw Dak and Sera grin at each other.

"Follow us," Sera said, standing up and grabbing Laika's leash. "They've got a lab set up in the barn. And we're going to help them test their latest invention."

"We are?" Riq asked. "Wait. What are you two up to?"

"Riq, Riq, Riq," said Dak. He put an arm around the older boy's shoulder. "Let me ask you a question: Why would anybody want to study history when they could live it?"

"What was all that about learning your lesson?" he asked pointedly. But he grinned as he asked it.

"We did learn a lesson," Dak said. "Stick together."

"And when it comes to history: Look, don't touch," Sera added.

"What's the worst that could happen?" Dak asked. He squeezed Riq's shoulder and ran ahead to join Sera.

Riq watched Dak, Sera, Arin, and Laika start toward the barn together. He was torn. Mere moments ago, he'd been ready to leave the life of adventure behind him. To settle down. Be a normal kid again.

But he had never really been a normal kid, had he? None of them had.

Sera turned around. "You coming?"

He rubbed his shoulder, then smiled, setting off toward the door that Sera was holding open for him.

THE END

Infinity Ring • Episode 8
HYSTORIAN CHALLENGE

You've gone up against some of the toughest villains in history. But your greatest challenge might be your friends! See how you measure up against them when the Hystorians put you to the test.

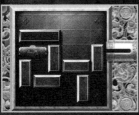

Consider your next move!   Race to the finish!

Do you have what it takes to be one of the greats? Log on now to find out!

Fix the past. Save the future.
scholastic.com/infinityring

"Come on," Dak said anxiously. "They're just about to issue their verdict. You do your thing, and I'll keep an eye out for unwanted guests." He stopped her near the back row of chairs and transferred the translation device, which was gold like the Ring, from his ear into Sera's. She felt the translator in her tooth, which Riq had inserted months ago, spark to life once the earpiece was in place. Dak winked at her—which was weird—and stepped back into the shadows just as one of the cardinals slammed his gavel against the table.

"We have our verdict," the man said in Italian.

Sera could understand him perfectly now. It was a little gross to think of Dak's earwax mixing with her own, but it was the only way she'd be able to present her argument.

"By majority vote," the cardinal went on, "we find the defendant, Galileo Galilei—"

"Wait!" Sera said, leaping out from behind the last row of chairs.

Everyone spun around to look at her. The courtroom was packed. She stepped forward, trying to appear confident, and stated, "Galileo is right about the heliocentric theory, and I can prove it!"

Two of the guards came rushing into the courthouse and took Sera by her arms, but one of the cardinals stood up and shouted, "Let the girl speak!"

Sera saw that while the rest of the cardinals were dressed in traditional cassocks, the robe of the man who'd just spoken up had gold trim, like the men outside. She wondered if he was part of the AB group, too.

When the guards released her, Sera walked down the aisle toward the front of the proceedings, feeling as nervous as she'd ever felt in her entire life. She scanned the crowd for her parents. Hadn't Dak said they were here somewhere? Then she saw Galileo was looking right at her. It was a dream come true to be able to defend him. But that dream would quickly turn into a nightmare if she failed.

One of the guards tried to take the dog out of the courtroom, but the cardinal wearing the gold trim came to Sera's defense a second time. "Leave the dog alone," he said. Then he turned to Sera. "Please, go on, young lady. Tell us why you believe Galileo is correct in his assertion that the Earth does indeed revolve around the sun. As you know, the church contends it's the other way around."

Sera stepped in front of the row of cardinals and cleared her throat. She looked back at Galileo. She could see it in his eyes: He was counting on her. But what she was about to do was more complex than he knew. Aristotle was the one who helped establish the geo-centric theory—which stated that all the other planets, and the sun, too, revolved around the Earth. Sera felt really weird about proving the founder of the Hystorians wrong about something. But hadn't Aristotle also claimed that science and knowledge were ever evolving?

Sera's dog trotted up to her and sat down, her tongue lapping out the side of her mouth. Sera petted her and took a steadying breath. She then turned her attention toward the cardinals. "Are any of you familiar with a man named Sir Isaac Newton?" she asked.

The men all shook their heads.

"That's because he doesn't live anywhere around here," Sera said. "And he refuses to travel to Rome. But a few days ago, I had the good fortune of speaking to Mr. Newton. And I believe some of the things he told me will change astronomical science forever."

When the men all leaned forward, seemingly intrigued by her opening, Sera knew she'd have just this one chance to explain it in a convincing manner. And she knew she'd have to keep it simple enough for everyone in the entire courtroom to understand.

She took another deep breath, let it out slow, and began.

She told the men how Isaac Newton was walking in a garden one day when he witnessed an apple falling from an apple tree. It was a normal-enough occurrence, sure, but it got him to thinking. Why had the apple fallen toward the ground instead of falling sideways or rising straight up in the air? Why was the fruit seemingly attracted to the ground? And why did it happen the same way every time?

When Isaac Newton thought more about this event, Sera told the courtroom, he had an epiphany. When released from any height, all earthly objects fell toward the ground. He even tested his theory. And then he took it a step further, suggesting that *every* object draws other objects toward it, but the larger and heavier object always possesses the more powerful drawing power. Therefore the apple will always fall toward the Earth instead of the Earth rising up toward the apple.

To state it simply, Sera explained, the Earth is a million times heavier than an apple, therefore its drawing power is a million times stronger.

Sera swallowed and looked around the room.

Dak was nowhere to be found.

But Galileo was nodding in support. And the cardinals were all still listening.

She went on.

"Sir Isaac Newton then applied this idea in a more universal way," she told them. "If the sun is a million times larger and heavier than the Earth, which Mr. Galileo has observed in his extensive telescopic research, then isn't it going to have a draw that is a million times stronger?"

When nobody said anything, she answered her own question. "Of course it is. And that's what causes the Earth to revolve around the sun instead of the other way around. It has nothing to do with politics or religion and everything to do with science."

A rumbling of voices started spreading through the courtroom.